CW01085311

"Bellamy is David Lynch in print sandpaper jumpsuit sandy side i hints for the less pop-culturally studying poop up close in the toi class, and hopelessness, all magnified ..... funny, post-feminist glare. This is the Punk Aesthetic."
—Lynn Breedlove,
author of Godspeed: A Novel

"Pink Steam is a compulsive read. This expert collection of essays qua fictions walks a vertiginous border between individual experience and the sadistic force of the accepted 'norm.' There is truth on one side, lying on the other. Then they switch, the inanimate become the animate, the fiction reality, and what seemed peaceful and clean suddenly becomes monstrous. Barbie's Dream House turns gothic, Judy Garland sadly ponders Henry Darger, a woman in Florida turns into a reptile, demons are exorcised via bulimia, and so on. No weird world this, but rather the vanishing middlebrow America of Montgomery Ward's, Filter Queen vacuums, all beef franks, and King Kong. Yet for all that Pink Steam is not kitschy, it is a culturally astute document of the real written by a master at the height of her powers."
—Jennifer Moxley,
author of Imagination Verses **and** The Sense Record

"In Pink Steam, one sentence eviscerates another the way Regan cried for help on the surface of Linda Blair's skin. Bounding from autobiography to Oscar Wilde to King Kong to the booze-addled body of Judy Garland, Dodie Bellamy's anarchic imagination sends the cozy pieties of linguistic form through a blender, suturing the results into something perversely original. If anyone can drag the sleeping, stagnant beast of contemporary literature into the future, she can."
—Brian Pera,
author of Troublemaker

"Dodie Bellamy may well be America's answer to Roland Barthes."
—Steven Shapiro,
Washington Review of Books

PINK STEAM

Dodie Bellamy

PINK STEAM

Dodie Bellamy

suspect thoughts press
www.suspectthoughtspress.com

Copyright © 2004 by Dodie Bellamy

Cover image and design by Shane Luitjens/Torquere Creative
Book design by Greg Wharton/Suspect Thoughts Press

First Edition: June 2004
ISBN 0-9746388-0-3

Library of Congress Cataloging-in-Publication Data

Bellamy, Dodie.
  Pink steam / by Dodie Bellamy.
    p. cm.
  ISBN 0-9746388-0-3 (pbk.)
  I. Title.
PS3552.E5319P56 2004
813'.54--dc22

2004000942

Suspect Thoughts Press
2215-R Market Street, PMB #544
San Francisco, CA 94114-1612
www.suspectthoughtspress.com

Suspect Thoughts Press is a terrible infant hell-bent to publish challenging, provocative, stimulating, and dangerous books by contemporary authors and poets exploring social, political, queer, spiritual, and sexual themes.

Work Cited in "Can You Hear Me Major Tom?"

SPACE ODDITY
Words and Music by David Bowie
© Copyright 1969 (Renewed) Onward Music Ltd.
London, England
TRO - Essex Music International, Inc., New York
Used by Permission

Works Cited in "Delinquent"

Kathy Acker, *My Mother: Demonology*, Grove Press, 1994. All subsequent indented or italicized passages are from this manuscript. In two of the paragraphs I string together unrelated lines from Acker's novel. With the kind permission of Matias Viegener, executor for the estate of Kathy Acker.

Carol Clover, *Men, Women, and Chain Saws: Gender in the Modern Horror Film,* Princeton University Press, 1992.

Maya Deren, *Divine Horsemen: The Living Gods of Haiti,* McPherson & Company, 1983.

G.B. Jones Retrospective, ed. Johnny Noxzema, The G.B. Jones Foundation, 1992.

Linda Williams, *Hard Core: Power, Pleasure, and the "Frenzy of the Visible,"* University of California Press, 1989.

Special thanks to Cedar Sigo for research assistance.

I would like to thank the following publications, presses, and editors for their generous support in publishing earlier versions of the pieces in this collection: *Best American Erotica 2001*, Susie Bright; *Bombay Gin*; *Boo*, Deanna Ferguson; *Bottoms Up* catalog, Robert Glück; *City Lights Review*; *Democracy the Last Campaign*, Margaret Crane and Jon Winet; *Errant Bodies*, Matias Viegener; *Fascination: The Bowie Show* catalog, Wayne Smith and Rex Ray; *Feminist Studies*, Rachel Blau DuPlessis; *Farm*, Hudson; *Five Fingers Review*; Hanuman Books, Raymond Foye; *Interruptions*, Tom Beckett; *Low Blue Flame*, Brian Pera; Meow Books, Joel Kuszai; *Moving Borders: Three Decades of Innovative Writing by Women*, Mary Margaret Sloan; *Nest: A Magazine of Interiors*, Matthew Stadler; *Non*, Laura Moriarty; *PIECE! 9 Artists Consider Yoko Ono* catalog, Rick Jacobsen and Wayne Smith; *A Poetics of Criticism*, Juliana Spahr, Mark Wallace, Kristin Prevallet, and Pam Rehm; *Semiotext(e) USA*; *Shiny International*, Michael Friedman; SUNY Buffalo Poetics listserv colloquium on gender and writing, Chris Alexander; Talisman House Publishers, Ed Foster; *Tiny Shoes* catalog, Darrell Alvarez; *Tripwire*, David Buuck and Yedda Morrison; *Walrus*; *Zyzzyva*, Howard Junker.

for Kevin and my mother

Her breath is quickened notably, flanks pumping, nostrils wide and pink. Steam rises from damp curls of fur.

—*A Spark in the Dark,* LotR fan fic by Zoe (aka Luinëturiel)

Contents

Barbie's Dream House

In the tight framing of David Levinthal's close-ups there is no human — or doll — body to establish a sense of scale. The Dream House loses its status as miniature, and we the viewers lose our identity as the big ones. We are thrust inside the Dream House. The sofa will seat two of us. From our Barbie's eye view, the bed seems kind of short — our permanently high-heeled feet would hang off the end. This bed, taut as an Army cot, and oddly sized, midway between a twin and a double, announces our sexual ambivalence. I imagine walking through Barbie's living room feeling off-kilter as I did in the '70s when I took acid and ambled through my own apartment looking at all the toys — kaleidoscope, hookah, waterbed, stereo, Silly Putty, wire whisk — thinking how thoughtful, how kind of this Dodie person to acquire these marvelous things for my pleasure. The objects felt slightly smaller than usual or I was slightly larger, an oaf moving through someone's stage set. The cheap cardboard walls are those of postwar prefab housing. My father was a union carpenter, and the two things he railed against the most were scabs and prefab houses. I remember him ramming his fist against our thick plaster walls and declaring that if this were a prefab wall his fist would have gone right through it! Now that I'm in them, Barbie's dreams seem rather modest, flimsy.

This Dream House, Barbie's premiere Dream House, was manufactured in 1962, and the sharp corners of its streamlined furniture mirror the creamy angularity of Barbie's body. Barbie's only been around for three years. Her arms and legs are not yet bendable, her lips are perched in a sophisticated, decadent pout. (She will not smile until 1976). Her favorite outfit is "Gay Parisienne": in white cats'-eye sunglasses and red chiffon scarf Barbie leans against a shadow-crazed wall, mysterious and dangerous as a spy in a Stanley Donen film, her gigantic red and white striped breasts pointing straight to Russia. 1962 — the Cuban Missile Crisis, the Kennedys, Khrushchev, freedom riders, student sit-ins, Timothy Leary discovers LSD, hootenannies, the U.S. Army occupies Saigon,

American astronauts enter outer space, Marilyn Monroe and Hermann Hesse die, *On the Road* is sanitized on TV's *Route 66*, Findhorn and Esalen are founded. None of this infiltrates the Dream House, except obliquely, like voices whispering in a novel by Robbe-Grillet. On the console TV, the same picture day after day, always the cartoon woman with the phallic shaped object floating beside her head.

Abandoning the neutral color schemes mandated by bourgeois decorators, the Dream House's insistence on gold, magenta, and cobalt hints at a disquieting bohemia. Framed abstract art dots the living room wall. In the more naturalistic painting beside the bed, an exotic mosque-like turret looms above the tricycle in the foreground. Nat King Cole's jazzy *Love Is the Thing* is tossed across the coffee table. A hutch holds twenty-five hardcover volumes. I can't read the titles, but I imagine they're classy with an edge: *Franny & Zooey, Ship of Fools, Sex and the Single Girl, Fail Safe, Youngblood Hawke*. Leatherbound Great Books editions—no trashy pocketbook *The Carpetbaggers*. This is a Dream House in which martinis are consumed—in martini glasses.

Details accrue to suggest a life. But whose? Barbie's name is on the box, so it must be hers. But what kind of life does Barbie lead? Sophisticated, suburban, vapid? Does Barbie ever read those provocative books above her bed? And what about those college banners? Their false naïveté seems kinky amidst all this sophistication. The longer you stare at it the tenser the Dream House makes you feel. Props keep shifting just beyond the periphery of your vision. From photo to photo the pancake pillows move about the bed. In one scene two of them have leapt to the sofa. At first Ken's portrait is prominently displayed on the console stereo. But when we blink our eyes, he's been exiled to the empty closet. Nat King Cole moves from coffee table to the console, which is now open, revealing a big hole with a turntable at the bottom. The cartoon woman, as always, seems satisfied; as always the phallic object floats to her right. The blue ottoman from the bedroom has joined her. Ken has evaporated from view. Who rearranged these accessories? Barbie seems remarkably absent. (Where *are* her clothes?) Is some voyeuristic giant looming just offstage with a hand as big as King Kong's? Or is the Dream House a magnet for poltergeist activity? Barbie's adolescent sexual secrets burst through cardboard dimensionality and things fly about. Barbie, the all American girl, is based, it is said, on a German pornographic doll, Bild Lilli. Barbie and Ken are really brother and sister, named after the children of their creators, Ruth and Elliot Handler. Incest, pornography, Euro-decadence...what next? I never owned a Barbie, but I touched one, pulled down the top of her swimsuit and rubbed her rock hard breasts with my thumb. The yellow puddle beside the bed is a trapdoor—it opens, whooshes me to The Basement.

In the center of the back wall, resting on a built-in vanity, a tinfoil mirror reflects and distorts, reflects and distorts. This mirror is the only thing in the house that doesn't look biodegradable, a shiny bit of stuff I imagine a bird weaving into her nest, its silver surface reflecting the room back on itself. I remember my wobbly reflection in the rest room of a mental hospital. It's 1962, in fact—I'm eleven years old, visiting my uncle. My mother tells me the mirrors are metal so the patients can't hurt themselves. Next to the rest room is a beauty parlor, and this is very confusing to me. I can't imagine being crazy and getting my hair done, sitting in one of those barber chairs and looking in the mirrors at my warped lopsided perm. Once you're inside the Dream House, the ground keeps shifting and shifting... In the distance we hear the clicking of Barbie's high heels—she's stalking us in her black and white striped swimsuit—so mysterious, so foreign—a zebra with thick kohl-lined eyes.

You Edju

Each morning when I open my eyes the first thing I see is Caitlin Mitchell-Dayton's Judy Garland pinned to the side of my armoire. A long pale yellow rectangle, pale brown pine grain lapping its sides, wavy as a dream dissolve. Judy stands in the middle in her famous hobo outfit, aging, bloated, taking a break. She's the size of a well-fed house cat. Her left hand rests on her hip, her right hand holds a cane and a cigarette. Her right leg crosses her left at the knee, the toe of her combat boot touching the "ground." Another, slightly higher positioning of Judy's bent leg has been whited out. Did Caitlin change her mind—or is this some past movement that Judy herself can never fully eradicate? Judy is a woman with an intricate shadow, a gold puddle crisscrossed with bronze lines that form diamonds, silver circles at the intersections, black dot in the center of each circle. Once again verisimilitude goes down the tubes. Judy looks very tired. Her head hangs to the right, her full lips are relaxed, parted, her heavy lidded eyes are cast downward. She's thinking to herself, wondering what "outsider art" really means. Is it merely talent that unwinds "outside" the art establishment—or does one have to be a weirdo? Judy's thoughts turn to the Henry Darger show. "Outsider Art," it said in bold black letters, right there on the wall of the old Chicago public library. She's glad she saw Darger's illustrations of hermaphroditic war-torn children in his hometown, midweek, in the loneliness, the eeriness of an empty hall. Whenever she turned her back to them, the children snuck away from the cataloged voyeurism of the gallery, reverted to the unseen, cluttered limbo of a janitor's bedroom. Judy exhales a big puff of smoke, her chest deflates for a moment then floats back up. Darger's watercolors remind her of Raymond Pettibon's work, more of a spiritual kinship than a specificity—the lack of formal training, the cultural infusions, startling convergences, the whole image/text thing, the hyperintelligent primitivism, obsessiveness, the narrative impulse, the volume. Fame hasn't brought Raymond much happiness. She's often thought he'd feel more comfortable with Darger's life, isolated, unknown, amassing these thousands of images in his tattered Hermosa Beach home. That's what he expected for himself, she's sure of that.

Jeweled winged creatures come to rescue Darger's children. If Darger's children are life, the winged beings are larger than life, pale humanoid butterflies as tall as the paper they're rendered on, languorously poised to battle the weather, their multicolored wings beacons against impending storm clouds. Judy raises a finger to trace their outlines. She can see herself reflected in the protective glass, can feel the children suffocating beneath it. A museum guard appears beside her, says, "How did you get in here with that coffee? You'll have to take it outside." *Outside of what* she wonders.

In the living room at Hermosa Beach a cat sat on a table, I bent down to pet it, "Hi kitty!" It bit my arm, not a little love bite, but viciously. Fortunately I was wearing a jacket. When I fled to the kitchen Raymond gave this embarrassed not-again sigh. "It bit you? Damn." The cat, he explained, used to belong to a Brazilian movie star. His brother's girlfriend rescued it from veterinary death row, where it was being used as a blood donor for better-socialized pets. The cat clawed the star's face so badly she had to have plastic surgery. I was spending the weekend with Raymond and his mother in their two-story stucco house. Also staying there were Raymond's brother and his girlfriend and some other guy. I never figured out who the other guy was, but he was in trouble, I got that much. I gathered that people were always coming and going. I slept in Raymond's studio, in a cot with racks of his drawings so low above me I could barely sit up. I enjoyed being stacked beneath all that art, imagined the papers flapping and fluttering, navigating my dreams. Raymond showered me with money, so much money I finally barked, "Raymond, stop trying to buy love!" But the money meant so little to him, he had pockets full of it, I did take some. I like money. We talked endlessly over martinis, brunches, dinners, red wine. "Gratuitous sex and violence," I remember him saying, "I have no problem with that." Raymond's mother told me grisly stories of the Russian invasion of Estonia, how she fled in a German ship as the Russians opened fire. She's still beautiful, looks twenty years younger than her eighty-some years, eats health foods and jogs every morning. And such a keen mind. She told me about Raymond's ancestors, his childhood, his IQ score so high the school insisted on a second testing. I felt comfortable there with Raymond and his mother, not like a guest — more like I was absorbed. Their limitless generosity was beautiful, but rather startling. Raymond's mother also told me his faults, all of them, as if she were trying to win me over, to have me all to herself. Or maybe she was trying to scare me away. I don't know. I felt like if I wanted to — and part of me did want to — I could stay there forever, eventually people might complain, might say I was bad news, dangerous, but as with the psychopathic cat nobody would bother to oust me. The cat was like Fate. Who has the momentum . . .

I was raised in Hammond, a working class suburb of Chicago. In the industrial Midwest of my youth, strong lines were drawn between inside/outside, normal/abnormal, natural/freak — and those lines were brutally enforced. In high school I was a lesbian, i.e., on the wrong side of all those slashes. I was terrified of anybody finding out — especially because of Edju Tucker. Edju went to a high school on the other side of town. I never saw him. I didn't need to. Edju was a legend. Carloads of teenagers would drive past Edju's house honking their horns and yelling, "Hey Edju!" On a good night, Edju would dart onto the front lawn and bare his ass. Edju was said to suck cock, and all the kids would jeer at one another, "You Edju," meaning, "You queer." Edju was a punching bag, a blob of flypaper snagging jock fist after jock fist, but I never knew if he actually existed, as more than a (sub)urban legend, an object lesson of what would happen if "they" found out you were queer — until 1997, when I flew home for my father's funeral where, for the first time, my brother and I really talked. In 10th grade, I learned, Joey fell in with a bad crowd — drug dealers and car thieves. Our parents "did some job of raising kids," he joked. "I'm a convicted felon, and you're weird." Joey was particularly close to one dealer named Cindy, for whom he used to hold money, thousands of dollars at a time. Cindy introduced Joey to Edju Tucker. I felt this *Big Chill* frisson at the mention of Edju's name. "Oh yeah?" I said casually. "What's he been up to?" Edju, Joey told me, is now a 300 pound drag queen who works with caustic chemicals at the sanitation department, and the fumes have burnt out his nostrils. Joey refers to Edju as "it." "So now it can't smell anything." Edju still likes to suck cock, won't let anybody touch his body. Cindy, Edju's only friend, died a few years ago. These days not even the high school kids bother with him. Edju pangs my heart. I wish I could be his John Waters and crown him the new Divine. I imagine treasures inside his apartment, wherever it is, hidden among his huge gowns and chipped coffee cups. I hope they're there. A magical realm of winged children without noses, of winged cocks dying to be sucked.

Judy's cigarette burns down, singes her fingers. She doesn't bother to move.

Complicity

In Medias Res

After midnight in Lizzie's Sonoma county studio apartment, a garage converted into a ski loft: beamed ceiling, redwood walls, and funnel-shaped fireplace. On the radio, a phone-in psychologist. Lizzie nervously sets down her lemon grass tea, a fluted cup with roses, and calls. "I have this problem, you see, I uh shoplift. Compulsively."

The radio psychologist tells Lizzie that stealing is a substitute for love.

Things Lizzie Has Stolen for Me

1. Two 100% cotton knit tops, multicolored nubby boat neck and smooth cream scooped with large buttons down the front. The tiny curtained cubicle, I have tried on four things, the ones I want disappear down Lizzie's tan pants. Then she switches the 4 item tag with a 2 item one that happens to be in her purse. Standing in the hall so the clerk is sure to hear, she yells, "Hurry up, I'll meet you in the car."

2. One facial mask, with Elastin, crushed almonds and thyme, a woman's naked shoulder on the label. A health food store, in full view of the clerk, it falls into her pocket.

3. A purple sash, rayon from India. At Cost Plus nobody monitors the dressing rooms. Child's play.

Lizzie fills her purse with socks and chemises and pepper mills.

All she has to do is get some love and then she'll stop.

4. Romika clogs, tan leather with low rubber heels, my Christmas present. While I ask the saleslady questions about

jewelry, Lizzie is to my right stuffing them in her purse. "Those little cuffs there, how do you get them over your ears?"

Outside on Castro Street, walking swiftly (but not too fast) we make a great team like Robert Redford and Paul Newman. We could dye my hair brown to blend in.

5. One chocolate truffle, Amaretto creme. Lizzie pokes through the cellophane and pops it in my mouth.

The writing flows or gets stuck. Lizzie and I have never had sex, not even at the mud baths in Calistoga. We've slept together a few times out of necessity—her apartment is cold and there's only one down comforter, it's pale rose with tiny white petals or leaves. Once her hand went between my thighs but she was sleeping.

True friendship is sharing the forbidden.

Each theft allowed Lizzie to breathe for a moment at the surface. The sweat on her lip, the racing heart provoked a state akin to religious moods.

Five foot six, shoulder-length black hair, size eight shoe and dress, Lizzie holds a tortoiseshell compact three inches from her face: brown liner, black lashes, dab of gray shadow. A warm creamy complexion inherited from her Mexican parents. No lipstick, she outlines her mouth with a brown pencil. Lizzie's clothes: khaki, black, gray, beige, a rare blue or red.

My husband is in the shower, I shout through the curtain, "I know you don't like it but I've got to put you in my piece. What name do you want?" "Fire Hose." "Come on—how about Jorge?" "What's this Jorge? I want Fire Hose."

And then there was the time with Fire Hose. He and Lizzie were raised in the same Chicago neighborhood, the same high school, but met out here through me. A Dickens coincidence. Fire Hose calls her Lizard and squeezes her cheeks. She makes fun of his Spanish. "Do you know what Puerto Ricans call a bus? A wawa! For the dog on the side of a Greyhound, like bow wow, a wawa!" Fire Hose was driving his cab that night, Lizzie said, "Let's get into bed and talk, it's more comfortable." Both of us in flannel nightgowns, we continue with the life of Edie Sedgwick. "Dodie, I'm going to sleep here, just 'til Fire Hose comes home." At six in the morning I tell her to move over. Three in a king-size bed, it's easy, both of them asleep and me in the middle: how far am I willing to share?

6. A can of Pure Maple Spread from Quebec. Safeway's fish-eye mirrors.

When Fire Hose and I got together he had moved back to the old neighborhood, so I spent a couple of months down the street from Lizzie's birthplace. A year in San Francisco's Mission District had not prepared me for this level of poverty, men sleeping in restaurant boiler rooms. My memory is full of dust and gravel, "Villa Lobos" scrawled everywhere.

Everything is bound to break wide open.

Lizzie calls her favorite method "exchanging." Step 1: Buy the cheapest item of clothing available. Step 2: Hide the item on your person and return to the store. Step 3: Take five items into a dressing booth. Switch the item you really want with the hidden one. Step 4: Return five items to the attendant and walk out.

Get caught? A racetrack driver could get killed, does that keep him off the track? A bank robbery at the movies, this masked James Dean holding the room on the tip of his rifle. Can you imagine a Chicana up there pocketing a jar of face cream at Merrill's?

Bodega Bay, clam chowder and plate glass, we sit at a table watching sea gulls. Lizzie has a problem—she is content to hang around the house not doing anything in particular. Her response to my "What's wrong with that?": "You should talk, you with your writing and your intellectual friends." I butter my sourdough. "Listen, writing alone won't do it. Some of the unhappiest people I know are writers. And they don't make that good of friends, not like you and Fire Hose. Did they really film *The Birds* here?"

Polk Street, a local schizophrenic, the kind you can smell half a block away, leaning over a trash can, shouting into the dark part, "You made a big mistake You made a big mistake You made a big mistake You made a big . . ."

The Strand, I pay as Lizzie sneaks through the turnstile: the teenage hitchhiker doesn't have a goal either, a little blonde visiting this movie from *Dallas*. Then she's moving to Los Angeles to study with a world famous sculptor. She sticks her thumb out on the way to receive it all. Finally, the homicidal maniac, I've been waiting ever since the previews. She smashes him in the face with a piece of art, it is large and lumpy. The terrified murderer lets her out and screeches down the highway.

I could have stabbed him with my fountain pen.

Lizzie feels an extraordinary calm at the moment of theft. Outside a jeweler's window, she doesn't think she will steal. No sooner does she get inside than she's sure she'll come out with a jewel: a ring or handcuffs. This certainty is expressed by a long shudder which leaves her motionless.

Breaking her diet with a huge slice of German chocolate cake, Lizzie asks, "Doesn't the word 'complicity' sound like a woman's name?" I smile and steal a bite.

Catalog of Ancestors

1969. The summer I graduated from high school. The Calumet Region, affectionately called "Da Region" in gangster movies, Al Capone was its most famous resident, my father's hero. Officially Northern Indiana but really a blue collar suburb of Chicago, on the Kennedy you can drive to the Loop in half an hour. 1969, the summer of Ralph.

Ralph had the same strawberry blond hair, the same green eyes, pale rosy complexion. We were inseparable and everybody thought he was my brother.

I should say Ralph and Nance and I were inseparable. Nance, straight brown hair and wire rims, so skinny, lived down the street. She was my lover in high school and college. Really we'd been doing it since we were eleven but it had only been a year since we quit pretending to be asleep.

7. The back of a director's chair, brown, I lost mine when moving. Lizzie walks up to a display chair, wriggles off the back and opens her sweatered armpit.

Summer at home — sheer endurance, hanging around the house, sticky and irritable. Just breathing the air was equivalent to smoking seven cigarettes a day. Ralph and Nance and I together, not love, a matter of sanity.

From the beginning we pooled our resources. Nance and I fried hamburgers at minimum wage, she at Nifty Burgers and I at A&W. Ralph wrote bad checks, supplemented by shoplifting. We worked well together. Nance and I would pay for Ralph's movie, afterwards he'd write a check for pizza. Nance and I'd buy a package of buns, Ralph would stick the ground beef down his pants.

Suddenly Kroger's and Sears became exciting.

Lizzie went to high school on Chicago's South Side during the Martin Luther King riots. Black girls carried scissors in their purses eager for a lock of blonde hair to show off, like a scalp. Every bathroom was a war zone. Lizzie smiles over her burrito, "That was one time I was glad to be brown."

Ralph had four sisters and a brother, all redheads. His older sister kept a list of the men she slept with, beside each name was a date and rating. Apparently this catalog filled several pages. His parents were divorced, the mother an alcoholic who cussed in a Southern accent. She had sex on the living room couch, the same one the twins peed on.

Instead of lemonade, Lizzie and her sister sold used Mexican lottery cards for a penny a piece.

A year of college under his belt and therefore world-wise, Ralph was plotting our corruption. He majored in French, so we started with Genet and de Sade. The three of us in cutoffs, sweating like crazy despite the fan. Nance and I sprawled across the floral bedspread, Ralph at my French Provincial desk, Simon and Garfunkel above his head. He reads out loud:

Ah, dear Eugénie, did you but know how delicate is one's enjoyment when a heavy prick fills the behind, when, driven to the balls, it flutters there, palpitating; and then, withdrawn to the foreskin, it hesitates, and returns, plunges in again, up to the hair! No, no, in the wide world there is no pleasure to rival this one: 'tis the delight of philosophers, that of heroes, it would be that of the gods were not the parts used in this heavenly conjugation the only gods we on earth should reverence!

Ralph lays the book down and licks his lips, "Well, what do you two think of that?" "Wow, Ralph, it's really neat."

8. One clear plastic purse studded with rhinestones. Courtesy of the toy department at Thrift Town. I keep my little plastic animals in it.

In grade school Lizzie and her sister would shine a flashlight on the wall, pretending they were at the drive-in. Then they'd put a plastic bag between their mouths and practice making out.

Needing petty cash, Ralph stole a can of Lemon Pledge from the corner Walgreens. Then he forged his mother's signature to a note requesting a refund. Half an hour later his little sister was back with the money.

At the same Walgreens they posted a list of all the people who'd written bad checks. When Ralph's name appeared for all the neighbors to see, his mother nearly went insane with rage. Then she found the letter where he admitted being gay, he hadn't even told his college girlfriend yet, and his mother kicked him out. That's how he started sleeping in Nance's Hungarian grandmother's basement for $25 a month.

Nance and I had never talked to a gay person before. Except the high school teachers, but they were always pretending. I couldn't deal with the women, the thought of growing up stiff and contained with a short ugly haircut was pure terror. Not for Nance, who fell in love with Judy Garland in kindergarten, she was looking forward to being a middle-aged dyke. She still is, except she teaches graduate school. It was easier with the men, I didn't have to become one. Especially my senior English teacher, it was rumored that in college he got down on all fours and howled at the full moon. I liked that.

9. A green vinyl footstool, rectangular with four buttons on top. The landlord had stored it in Lizzie's garage for a yard sale.

Ralph told us homosexuals wore mascara and picked each other up in cars. Then he described various sexual acts, using as many Latin names as possible. Nance and I had already tried a couple.

The further I progress, reducing to order what my past life suggests, and the more I persist in the rigor of composition the more do I feel myself hardening in my will to utilize, for virtuous ends, my former hardships. I feel their power.

When Lizzie was in the hospital, her sister slept with Lizzie's boyfriend. Not buying, not receiving. Taking.

Sitting on the front porch petting the dachshund, Ralph said, "You've got to go to college, it's your only way out." He made it sound great—drugs and parties and cutting classes.

And it was great. For all those reasons. But what a waste, after four years I graduated with honors and no idea how to support myself. My mother paid for it with kitchen work, mopping floors.

Really it was not big deal. Nance and I had been having sex for seven years but technically were virgins. Ralph was available. The day Nance's parents left on vacation we got drunk on sloe gin, spilling it all over the new kitchen cabinets. Whenever I hear the Beatles' *White Album* it all comes back. It was sickly sweet and red and sticky.

Climbing into Nance's bed, Ralph gave a brief lecture on penis size, then demonstrated. What I remember most is laughter: we knew this was a ridiculous situation.

We never did it again, and communal living continued as usual.

Sears will replace your paint if it doesn't cover. Lizzie and her sister want to do their bedroom so they buy half the amount needed, then take back the empty cans and complain about the pink showing through.

Ralph had been writing bad checks for two years, on three different accounts. He kept detailed records, could tell you to the penny how many thousands he owed. He seemed to actually enjoy reading all the threatening mail.

I stupidly told my mother about our financial arrangement. "How can you eat that pizza, knowing it was paid for with a bad check?" My mouth full of mushroom and pepperoni.

We knew we were perverts so we wallowed in it.

Ralph didn't give us any warning. One day he wrote the grandmother a check and disappeared. Nance and I were pissed. When it bounced we received the full brunt of her Eastern European Immigrant fury.

The last I heard of Ralph he was living in Indianapolis and had changed his name to Lee.

Legendary Materials

My personal weakness is sales. That's why I love Macy's—you can live your whole life through sales. All it takes is patience and the Sunday paper. You can buy it or visit one of San Francisco's many coffeehouses Sunday afternoon. There is always a copy of *Macy's California* lying around.

50% OFF CUBIC ZIRCONIUM—SWIVEL INTO G.E.'S 25" REMOTE COLOR CONSOLE AND SAVE!—COSMIC HEART WITH PEARL, REG. $100.00, SALE $67.00—YOUR CHOICE $12—25% OFF SELECTED LEOTARDS IN COMFY COTTON/SPANDEX BLEND

I had to wait three months for my red leather gloves, but it was worth it.

Every teak item is half-price except the wine rack Lizzie wants, so she peels a $20 pink sticker off a cheese saver and puts it on a wine rack. After paying, she uses the same sticker to buy another. Later both are returned to the Macy's in Sonoma at a $40 profit.

Fire Hose is sitting at the kitchen table when we get home, he doesn't know any of this. I say, "You should see the wine rack Lizzie just got, it was a *real steal*." She squints her eyes and hits me.

I take Lizzie to Old Wives' Tales, figuring feminist books can only do her good. She whispers, "Let's get out of her, I can't stand all these words." "Lizzie, these books were written for you." "No they weren't, they make me feel stupid." So we drive to Thrift Town instead.

10. One full slip, noncling apricot with minimal lace. A pink $4.99 sticker superimposed over the $22 tag.

Adrian, a friend of mine from work, tall, blond, well mannered, his father the vice president of a bank, far too antiseptic for my taste. Lizzie sees him at my kitchen table and is so attracted she runs into the bedroom. I follow. "What's the matter?" "He's so clean I feel like a cockroach."

It's the same with stealing—a touch of the magic wand and bam! She's a cockroach from 18th and Blue Island.

Lizzie has never slept with a Latino man.

11. One blue rolling ball pen. When I find mine in her purse, she pockets me a new one.

SAVE $40 ON THE ROYAL WITH FAST ONE-STEP CORRECTION

Church Street Station, Dos Equis in the food section, Michael in his pale skin and weathered leather jacket that once was brown. He used to steal food and books. I ask, "Did you need those things?" "Of course." "I mean, could you have gotten them otherwise?" "No." I lean back, shake my head, "That's not the same as doing it for sport."

Michael won't be that easily defeated. He pushes aside his glass and takes a drink from the bottle. He once knew a man who only wore white T-shirts. Whenever they got dirty, the man'd just go out and steal some more. That reminds me of Kevin, he does the same thing with thrift stores. Whenever his shirts get dirty, Kevin says, "It's time to do the laundry" and heads for the Salvation Army to buy a couple clean ones.

Michael is surprised, says he's seen Kevin in some pretty nice shirts. But he's holding his mouth that funny way, staring intently. This means Michael is thinking "Another Superficial Conversation." Soon he'll try to change the subject to something like structuralist literary theory. So I hold on to Kevin's clothes, innocently ask, "Don't you think that sometimes he could be a bit more choosy?"

A cockroach from 18th and Blue Island crawled out of Macy's with a $20 pepper mill on her back.

Writing about his job as a sheet metal worker, Michael uses "synchronicity," "semiotic," "metaphorical lever of exchange." I say, "Why the big words? You trying to sound smart or something?" He looks down the subway stairs then back at me. "I want to use a vocabulary I'm not even supposed to own."

PRO-MAGNALITE 11-PC. SET SALE $190 WITH BONUS

Taking out my Fast Pass I said, "Michael, that's a good story, I think I'll put it in my piece." He smiled, so I guess it's okay. I wouldn't want to be accused of stealing his life.

To me a friend is someone who raids my refrigerator without asking.

Imagine a roommate who marks an X on every egg.

Any tag with a green slash through it is half off. Lizzie immediately goes out and gets a matching green marker.

She finds a copy of Kafka's *The Metamorphosis* in my study, the light is on all night. Over coffee and scrambled eggs, a T-shirted Lizzie, no makeup: "Dodie, I am Gregor Samsa."

Three of the men I know are reading Derrida but none of them understand him. They admit this to me, not one another. Each time I hear the story my response is the same: "Don't you think that's part of his appeal, that he's incomprehensible?" Michael's the only one who sees my point.

Knowledge—something to be locked up? The only way to get it is like Michael, to steal.

Gregor Samsa crawled out of Thrift Town with a clear plastic purse on his back, it was studded with rhinestones and sparkled.

Lizzie wants to write a piece on shoplifting, to get it out of her system. I volunteer to help, suggesting scattered paragraphs, each one small enough to fit in your pocket, and nobody sure where anything comes from:

If I am accused of using theatrical props as fun fairs, prisons, flowers, sacrilegious pickings, stations, frontiers, opium, sailors, harbors, urinals, funerals, cheap hotel rooms, of creating mediocre melodramas and confusing poetry with cheap local color, what can I answer?

How much are you willing to put out for this?

$22.50 RAVIOLI HEAD

Lizzie has never talked to Michael, but she saw him once at my reading last summer. Afterward, driving down Valencia, she exclaims, "How can you control yourself around him, he's so attractive." "You don't know him, it's easy." Then I add, "He lived with a Mexican woman for eight years." Lizzie switches on the turn signal and for a moment looks hopeful.

No work for over a month, I think twice about buying a burrito. Lizzie has gone back to Sonoma. After two days with her I could own anything. Old Wives' Tales, a new book on female psychology, $16.95. They are so trusting here, so easy to slip it in my bag. How did this thought slip past my censor? Ripping off a feminist bookstore and me a woman writer, there could be nothing worse. I leave immediately, not trusting my hands, my mind.

FREE KNIFE SHARPENING

The atmosphere of the planet Uranus appears to be so heavy that the ferns there are creepers; the animals drag along, crushed by the weight of the gases. I want to mingle with these humiliated creatures which are always on their bellies. If metempsychosis should grant me a new dwelling place, I choose that forlorn plane, I inhabit it with the convicts of my race.

When I pay full price for something I feel defeated.

Lizzie gives her homeopath $80 for a kleptomania remedy. She just takes this white powder and avoids coffee and sugar for the next three months.

12. One Chemex coffeemaker, 4-cup capacity. This one's disputable. A month ago in Cost Plus she remarked how easily it would fit into her purse. When I get it for my birthday I ask if she bought it. Lizzie turns her back to me and chops onions, "Yes." "Come on, don't lie to *me*." "Dodie, leave me alone."

Can You Hear Me Major Tom?

"Space Oddity," with its catchy tune and stagy little space narrative, is surprisingly enigmatic, a poignant evocation of dystopic passivity. As he's bandied about by forces outside his control, Major Tom's fate is inevitable—the fixings for high tragedy were it not for his complacency. *Here am I floating round my tin can, far above the Moon.* Tom doesn't rail, he doesn't struggle, he merely drifts off, unplugged from marriage, fame, commodity culture. His rhymes are either singsongy or off (do/blue/moon), he's the Emily Dickinson of deep outer space. "Space Oddity" became my anthem in the summer of 1974 in Bloomington, Indiana, the summer I decided to be straight. I played it constantly as I broke up with my girlfriend, moved into a house with four gay guys, and started sleeping with a bisexual whom I thought gloriously handsome. My roommates were always bickering about that. "Michael McQuillan cute!" they'd snarl. "That closeted queen—I don't think so." "Closeted" meant he hadn't sleep with any of them.

Michael was blond, Irish, his features regular except one slightly roving eye that gave him an aura of the otherworldly. The night I met him he was hitting on my friend Ted. "You are so gorgeous," I drunkenly spewed at Michael. "And you know it!" To everyone's surprise he took me home instead of Ted. I loved his body, the way it stretched out naked, warm, smooth and long as taffy, long golden taffy. I loved to watch his cock spring up, dewy with youth and so grabbable. He was twenty-one, two years younger than me. In my tiny bedroom he rubbed my back with coconut scented lotion, and to this day whenever I smell coconut, I get all sentimental, overcome with an ambient eroticism I don't know what to do with. *And the stars look very different today.* My dresser was an ornate dark wooden antique, with bowed legs and embossed vines and flowers. Its frou-frouness inspired me to drape the bedroom with cloth, vivid floral curtains from the '40s, maroon brocade swatches, white embroidered runners, eyelet lace, doilies, a lavender Indian print bedspread—I hung the cloth across the window, over the top of the dresser, on the walls, and over my bed. The effect—half womb, half harem—was one my roommates loved. They were doubled up in the other two, normal-size bedrooms, so whenever I was out for the night, if they brought a trick home, they'd do it in my room, the "trick room." *And I think my spaceship knows which way to go.* I wasn't there that often and when I was I preferred to crawl in bed with Ken, the roommate I felt closest to, not for sex, he wouldn't have tolerated that, but I was frightened of sleeping alone. Halfway through the summer he said, "You can't do this anymore." "Why not," I whined. "Because I don't like it." "Come on, Ken, why do you have to be so mean, please!"

Major Tom's irrevocable isolation rhymed with my own displaced need for privacy. I couldn't stand to be alone, yet I didn't want anyone to witness my dailiness, an indiscriminate collage of fragments, random encounters. Like all young people I was trying to forge a life of nonstop grandiosity, but I felt disconnected, simultaneously affectless and overwrought. I loved the song's creepy sound effects, clashing with its power ballad surges, then morphing at the end into a flourish of eerie dissonance. Bowie suggests the uncanny in the duet he performs with himself, his two voices mingling, then separating, then drawn back together in shaky alignment. I didn't analyze the song, I sucked it in through my pores, said, "Yes." I'd put on the record and check out into a solitary erotic haze. The heat pours in through the windows. The light is so bright the room looks grainy. A group of us are lying down, on the mattress on the floor and on the floor itself, and I stare at the speakers with their black mesh covers, blown away.

That first night he picked me up, I sat in his kitchen impatient and confused as Michael insisted on making some popcorn with Italian seasonings. While he popped and slathered on butter, I kind of gave up on the sex, but after we ate our popcorn, it *did* happen, light and playful, puppy sex. I didn't come, the downside to being straight, but afterward Michael told me I was the first woman he'd ever slept with he didn't feel guilty about. "What about guys," I asked. "I never feel guilty about guys." Catholicism, I thought, is a very strange religion. Michael lived in a house, with a swimming pool, paid for by an English professor he was involved with. One morning as I sat up in bed beside his sleeping body, reading *Soul on Ice,* the English professor walked in. Cartoon eyeballs popping out, all around. Michael had a job at the post office that paid four times what I made on workstudy. He got it, he bragged, by sleeping with a financial aid officer. I knew the one he was talking about and couldn't imagine Michael's gleaming ass touched by such a greasy, revolting pig. No matter how many times I fucked him, Michael was unavailable. Foolish as I was, I knew that, and it broke my heart. My heart broke the minute he touched me. But I liked it when he spent those older guys' money on me. It made me feel sophisticated and trampy, like a gun moll.

I occasionally slept with other guys—guys that I found bland, unsatisfying in their un-Michaelness. I kept doing it because when cuteness called, I answered. We all answered. My roommates showed me how they picked up guys outside the Monroe County Library. During the day we went there to sit in their egg-shaped pod chairs, they had several of them on short pedestals, white ovals with red interiors that really looked like eggs, giant eggs with gaping mouths that swallowed you when you sat in them. We pretended the chairs were hatching us, our alien, sandal-clad legs dangling from their lower lips. *Now it's time to leave the capsule if you dare.* At night when the library closed, its sidewalk turned into Cruising Central. Gay guys came from all over town and languidly strolled around the building, their eyes scanning for contact. *Commencing countdown, engines on.* I'd been on that corner at night dozens of times, and I was amazed I'd never noticed this before, these lean, scraggly headed creatures moving beneath the streetlights in slow motion, inching around the library, over and over, on a treadmill of sexual anticipation.

I went barefoot whenever possible. At the most I'd slip on water buffalo sandals, thongs with a hoop around each big toe, the soles thin as the vinyl that spun and spun. I wore a maroon dress from the forties that belonged to my girlfriend's Hungarian grandmother, with nothing under it save a pair of nylon hipster panties, apricot or lime green. I liked the looseness of the dress, the way it slid over my breasts, it made me feel gaunt, though I was far from that. My hair hung to the middle of my back, bright strawberry, bangless, parted down the middle. Michael found me attractive, which meant, for those couple of months, I was attractive. I knew when he tired of me I'd plunge back into hideousness, I was terrified of that. The living room in our house was a mess, pizza boxes, books, clothes and records a foot deep, David Bowie's reedy voice *and I think my spaceship knows which way to go* quivering though the speakers, which by now had lost their mesh covers. I had to hop and tiptoe through all the junk to turn the album over. The turntable's cover was buried in the garbage and I leapt on top of it, screech of plastic cracking and me yowling, my food bleeding.

1974—I was over drugs, over acid rock. "Space Oddity" proposed an existential groundlessness at odds with rock's optimistic linearity. With rock you dropped a hit, headed out the door and miraculously ended up at a Jefferson Airplane concert, marveling at the alterity of your journey. With "Space Oddity" there's no destination at all, no place to arrive. A chord snaps and Major Tom free-floats in the void. *Planet Earth is blue and there's nothing I can do:* Bowie's tense fatalism and splendor spoke to my core. My life was a blur, but sometimes the blur would crystallize into lucid, amazing moments. Michael's body was one of those moments, his cock in such sharp focus it cut me. He was a drunk, so every date began with us getting loaded at the Bluebird. Michael would ramble on about history and journalism (he was a double major) to anybody who would listen, his lame eye roaming with excitement, and I would zone out, waiting for the last call so we could go back to his place and sloppy fuck. When he wasn't around I'd go out drinking with my roommates, there was always one of them ready to roar, and picking up guys, so I ended up wasted every night, and I wasn't eating much except when Michael was paying for it *take your protein pills and put your helmet on* and one afternoon I passed out on an ancient leather sofa in the student lounge. I was awakened by some old lounge monitor lady. "No sleeping in here!" I hadn't been home for a couple of days. When I opened my front door I was accosted by this horrid acrid smell, I followed it into my bedroom, the top of my dresser was burnt, the wood bubbled and scorched, the cloth on top of it and the one hanging from the wall behind it charred, their edges gnarled a ragged brownish charcoal. "Who burnt down my bedroom!" I shrieked. Ken emerged and said it was Phil. "He was having sex by candlelight and he fell asleep." His tone was complacent, very *get over it*, so I sat on my bed in my stinky room and cried. "I'll hitchhike to Florida," I vowed, "go stay with Dennis." *Liftoff*.

The Debbies I Have Known
(with Ken Clinger as Oscar Wilde)

The Beginning

I had noticed her at the bus stop, wearing a Russian-styled fur hat, her hands stuck into a matching muff. Chicago was having a particularly bad winter, still I had never before seen a grown woman, or child, for that matter, carrying a fur muff. It is amazing that we met. She was a secretary in Auditing and I was a photographer's assistant. In other words, we were eighteen stories apart. The snow was too deep for the buses to run, so Debbie and I found ourselves trudging together the five blocks to the Ravenswood El. She had noticed me in the cafeteria. I was the only person she had ever seen there reading a book.

We never touched when we slept together. It didn't matter. I was delighted to be in her bed.

Insanity ran in Debbie's family. Her grandmother died of brain cancer. The old woman had terrorized Debbie, locking her in a closet, yanking her hair out with a comb. Placed alone on a train that ended at her mortician uncle's, she knew her mother was having another nervous breakdown. Eight years old, with a corpse down the hall, waiting to hear a sudden rustle, the hollow wheezing of dead breath.

In person, Debbie resembled her mother; having the same elegant symmetry of form, the same delicacy of features, and the same blue eyes, full of tender sweetness. But, lovely as was her person, it was the varied expression of her countenance, as conversation awakened the nicer emotions of her mind, that threw such a captivating grace around her.

Debbie's face magnified in the brightly lit mirror. She copies Marilyn Monroe's eyes, exactly. The best eye makeup remover is cheap baby oil, the cheaper the better. To get the thinnest, evenest strip of eyeliner, dab some oil on a Q-tip, drag it lightly along the lashes.

> Oscar Wilde: That's the smile of a twenty-year-old. That's the kind that's 1930s.

> Rosemary Hallward: Yeah, she has a real 1930s look.

> OW: She would have been 1930s really pretty, in sense. At least if she looked like that.

> RH: If she was a little thinner.

> OW: Well, even then they could be sort of plump. Because it was the healthy, wholesome, American look.

Debbie and I took lunch together. Every day. We alternated between the cafeteria in the basement and the executive dining room on the 26th floor. Fluorescent lights and indigestion, hundreds of people dressed in Montgomery Wards clothes. Though we discussed our favorite topics, art, sex, religion, there was an underlying desperation to these meals, as if we were each responsible for the other's not jumping out a window, screaming.

Her mother had always warned her to pursue a career. Any woman who let's a man get her under his thumb is a fool. Then he leaves her when she's forty-five, and she ends up living in a trailer park in Georgia.

Debbie was the only woman to betray me.

White canopy bed, crystal perfume bottle, Mae West poster in a silver frame, black and white Marilyn, skirt blown in her face. Hundreds of books: leatherbound classics, history, romances, popular psychology. Stale scent of cigarettes.

I come to her apartment, whimpering about the cab driver. He acts so strange, never wants to hug me, and I'm supposed to wait around until *he* wants it, and when he does I'm supposed to play dead. Debbie listens calmly, takes a drag off her cigarette, nods: "They're all that way."

The Gospel According to Debbie

1. Orgasms are easy to come by. When offered a choice, take money. It lasts longer.

2. At all times be mysterious.

3. Mayonnaise is the best thing for soft hair.

Debbie never came during sex, but walking along the lake at sunset, mesmerized by its brilliant pink undulations, a sudden throbbing would swell between her thighs. With great difficulty she would continue to walk, suppressing the reflex to gasp. Despite Debbie's obvious distress, I envied her, the aesthetic intensity of it.

No one who had seen Debbie in her infancy, would have supposed her to be a heroine. Her situation in life, the character of her father and mother, her own person and disposition, were all equally against her.

Dipping a Q-tip in cheap baby oil, Debbie swears her grandmother killed her grandfather with carrot juice.

4. Learn to use your eyes. Practice in the mirror.

> OW: Those eyes. You can see that she would turn against you at any moment. Especially the eye on the right, doesn't that look like it could scrutinize you and tear you apart?

> RH: I'm surprised she has lipstick on. I don't remember her wearing lipstick. What about her clothes?

> OW: Well, her teeth aren't white, but whose are? Her

clothes are loose, showing she's dressed for comfort or she's trying to let people think she's really casual. Let me see, she likes stripes. She doesn't get out in the sun much, she's really white.

RH: Would you find her attractive?

OW: She looks coarse. No, she's too ballsy for me to like her.

RH: Do you mean her as a person or the way she looks?

OW: They're one and the same.

Water stains haunting her bedroom wall. Two weeks after Debbie moved in, the man upstairs committed suicide in his bathtub. She awakened to Niagara Falls. Her Romanian landlord rushing aimlessly about muttering Hail Marys and giving the sign of the cross, Debbie dialed the operator, "I need to speak to the Cook County Police," she said, "I've just found a body!"

As she returned toward her chamber, Debbie began to fear that she might again lose herself in the intricacies of the apartment building, and again be shocked by some mysterious spectacle; and, though she was already perplexed by the numerous turnings, she feared to open one of the many doors that offered. While she stepped thoughtfully along, she fancied that she heard a low moaning at no great distance, and, having paused a moment, she heard it again and distinctly.

Twenty-five years old, fresh from Michigan, Debbie was plagued with an indelible wholesome glow. It took four years of hard work to attain an air of decadence. She bought stiletto heels, dyed her hair bright blonde, copied Marilyn Monroe's face. Cup after cup of cheap coffee, watching hookers at Golden Nugget Pancake House, she learned to smoke and cuss.

OW: Her cigarette makes her look like someone

who'd hang out in bars. Yes, that's the look she has. That working class woman who hangs out in bars type person.

RH: I guess it's strange that in one picture she could have the healthy 1930s glow and then the next one she looks trashy.

OW: Actually, she looks five years older than the last picture. She looks like she's had five hard years.

5. Don't bother trying to carry on an intellectual conversation with them. That's not what they're interested in.

Once a man asked Debbie to walk on him with high heels. Rolling her eyes, she said, "I can't do that—I'll puncture your spleen."

Debbie has seen *Gone With the Wind* sixteen times. Her mother was an extra in it, a yellow blur in the ballroom scene.

I can't think of a single tragic heroine named Debbie. Romeo and Debbie, Anthony and Debbie.

Trembling came upon Debbie, as she ascended through the gloom. To her melancholy fancy this seemed to be a place of death, and the chilling silence that reigned confirmed its character. Her spirits faltered. "Perhaps," she said, "I am come hither only to learn a dreadful truth, or to witness some horrible spectacle; I feel that my senses would not survive such an addition of horror."

Stepping into a pair of blue stiletto heels she got on sale at Montgomery Ward, Debbie says, "The trouble with loving a man is that it destroys your creativity."

Debbie's boyfriend was a screenwriter. She loved him even though he didn't bring in much money and would occasionally dine with his kinky actor friends. One of them got his kicks from being buried alive. Debbie had felt that dark suffocation in her own canopy bed.

6. When in public always smile.

> OW: She's got a practiced smile. It's amazing because when you look at it close, it's too teethy. She should have her upper lip a little lower.

> RH: Yeah, but when people smile it's a motion thing.

> OW: But, she's got a very projected aura. She looks party party party.

Growing up fat in Michigan was living on the flip side, the football player you've been socialized to want always beyond your reach. Debbie's father's constant digs, yelling to her in the bathtub that it sounded like she was beaching a whale.

Broadway and Belmont. Red naugahyde booth, formica woodgrain tabletop, above her head orange and blue teardrop lamps. Muzak. Absently pouring nondairy creamer, Debbie studies the transvestite hooker in the next booth. Anorexic, silicone nipples sculpted beneath a turtleneck sweater, she drenches her french fries with ketchup. It looks like an accident victim heaped on her platter. Staring straight at Debbie's fleshy cheeks, she yells out to the pancake house, "I eat potatoes to gain back my weight."

7. Use deception at all times. That's the only way you'll get what you want.

Debbie went to a Seventh-Day Adventist college, where her pierced ears caused quite a scandal.

The owner of the dance studio was a fruitarian, alcohol and drugs were forbidden. We were to amuse ourselves, instead, with fresh oranges. Standing beside a huge pile of rinds, Debbie felt an immediate attraction to me because I used to sleep with her current boyfriend. Longhaired and wide-eyed, a bit too sweet for my taste, she told me about her ex-husband.

He was an incurable voyeur, had been caught in a woman's closet, with a knife, watching her undress.

Debbie had the messiest apartment I've ever seen. Books and clothes and *Cosmopolitan* magazines formed a solid mass across the floor. You had to tiptoe everywhere. Whenever I wanted to drink from one of her emerald goblets, I had to first scrub out half an inch of mold. Except when she lived with her gay boyfriend. Their apartment (minus Debbie's bedroom) was immaculate art deco. Like living in the middle of a showroom. Taking a drag from her cigarette, Debbie said she felt like Albert Einstein in Rita Hayworth's body.

Debbie's hair was the brightest living gold, and despite the poverty of her clothing, seemed to set a crown of distinction upon her head. Her brow was clear and ample, her blue eyes cloudless, and her lips and the molding of her face so expressive of sensibility and sweetness that none could behold her without looking at her as a distinct species, a being heavensent, and bearing a celestial stamp in all her features.

Brushing black mascara on her lower lashes, Debbie said: "You can go to Ellen G. White's heaven or Jesus' heaven. But, if you want a custom-made heaven, you'd better start figuring things out for yourself."

> OW: She'd be someone that I could joke around with, but I'd have to be very aware of every word I said.
>
> RH: Why?
>
> OW: Because I couldn't trust her.
>
> RH: Just from looking at this picture?
>
> OW: Uh huh.
>
> RH: And what would make you feel that?
>
> OW: She looks like she'll take everything you say and

run away and tell it to someone else. She'll smile as you tell it to her and she'll sneer as she tells it to someone else.

RH: I kept thinking about how whenever I would be talking to her and she was going to get together with somebody, she would never say, "Oh, I'm just going to get together with somebody." She'd go, "I *have* to go see Joe now. If I don't go, he'll be upset. It's so boring." I mean, everybody in the world but me was boring to her. And after a while I started wondering, you know, what she said to them when she had to get together with me.

8. Love is a myth and passion is short-lived.

Debbie xeroxed the formula for *True Confessions* stories. Any sin was permissible as long as it was followed by the suitable amount of suffering and/or punishment. We made a pact to submit.

I envied Debbie because my mother never told me how to handle a man.

Debbie was sleeping with the cab driver I used to sleep with, the one with the vasectomy whose first wife used to go on radio talk shows and discuss her childhood on Venus. Standing beneath a streetlight in Logan Square, Debbie felt a "deep spiritual connection" with the woman since her last lifetime was also spent on Venus. I am still amazed that a Chicago cab driver could find two women from Venus. It makes me wonder where I come from.

OW: She looks like she's from the farm.

RH: She is.

OW: If you look at her now as a farmgirl, she looks like a farmgirl, unsophisticated.

RH: Well, that totally contradicts everything else you've said about her.

OW: No it doesn't.

RH: How doesn't it? If she looks like an unsophisticated farmgirl, how could she look phony?

OW: Because of her eyes.

RH: How could her eyes look different? She was born with those eyes.

OW: No, no. It's the various gradations of squint.

Opening a tube of fire engine red lipstick, Debbie said my fear of serenity was really a fear of death. Any change in intensity is, in a sense, a death. She saw her entire life as a series of deaths.

The pattern was: passion and remorse or passion and vengeance.

My fiasco with the photographer. Debbie's nursing me through it almost made the pain worth it. She dressed me in a wonderful white flannel nightgown and fixed me some tea, not a regular cup, but ruby crystal. We chain-smoked till five in the morning, dissecting the violence of passion and laughing.

9. If he shits on you, never take him back. Somebody sticks a knife in your back, the next time they'll only twist it in deeper.

Her body was soft and pink and forbidden.

Carson's was the only store in the Loop to carry White Shoulders perfume. Debbie and I would ride the el there, specifically to spray a tester behind our ears. Then we'd walk to the women's lounge at Marshall Field's. Gray marble stalls, a huge expanse of mirror. Though I never wore lipstick, I would stand there with her and meticulously smear on the waxy red. Then to Berghoff's with its ancient oak paneling and German waiters for dark beer and sausages. Then back to the North Side to Hemingway's Moveable Feast for hot fudge sundaes. Melting coffee ice cream and that dark warm goo, we would smile at each other and sigh.

All of this occurs in the past, except this sentence.

During her afternoon break, Debbie sneaks down to the photo studio, and I take cheesecake pictures of her.

OW: Have you ever seen Martha Raye smile?

RH: I can't remember.

OW: She's the one who smiles and it's so plastic. This is more sincere than Martha Raye's, but it comes close. I mean, that's a practiced smile.

RH: It does, it looks like she'd be selling toothpaste.

OW: If you met her and she smiled like that, you would like her at first.

RH: So you think she's good at winning people?

OW: Yes, she can. From this picture, it looks like she could, if she wanted to, she could impress you as someone to like.

RH: She looks bubbly.

OW: Yes.

After we both called off work, we put on satin nightgowns and sat in Debbie's bed watching soap operas. Debbie smoked. The nightgowns were more important than the TV. We fantasized our hair in curlers, a man's shirt steaming on the ironing board.

Debbie busied herself with following the aerial creations of the poets; and in the majestic and wondrous scenes which surrounded her Michigan home—the sublime shapes of the mountains, the changes of the seasons, tempest and calm, the silence of winter, and the life and turbulence of Midwestern summers—she found amble space for admiration and delight.

My second public reading. Somehow it is the Modern Language Association. Over a hundred people, I don't deserve them, begin, anyway, with Debbie:

> Dearborn Street
> three a.m.
> where the man was murdered for drugs
> silver bullets beneath a full moon
> hey there foxy
> the way you will keep on walking
> right between his eyes

> RH: She will always survive.

> OW: Survival, but it's very superficial on her. This picture—here there's honest Rosemary and surviving Debbie. Now some people can have both of that. They can go down to the depths, they can be honest and still be friendly and sincere. But, these are the two different sides of it right here.

The Middle

10. If you want a friend, talk to women and gay men.

Her part-time job at the frame shop became a full-time obsession. She met a man there: twenty-nine, Greek ancestry, dark mustache drooping over full lip, an appealing touch of vulnerability, the last vestige of a fat childhood. Debbie knew he was gay, but it didn't matter. The tension between them was mounting. To everyone's surprise, he invited me over to smoke a joint. In the living room, a most incredible art deco cabinet, Grecian warriors carved on the doors. A few tokes later, he could have been an ax-murderer-rapist and it wouldn't have mattered. He must have sensed that. Why else admit his attraction to Debbie, an attraction he felt was hopeless. She was too naïve, he could never take her to the bars, introduce her to his friends. I didn't want to leave, he was so honest, had such good taste. But Debbie was waiting for me at the frame shop, white angora kitten above her head. I told her how her mother's advice had backfired. "Dammit," she said, "damn."

"I am that god," he said, "who measures out the path of the long year, who sees everything, and by whose light the earth sees all. I am the eye of the universe, and, believe me, I am in love with you!" Debbie was afraid. In her fear, cigarette and lighter dropped from her nerveless fingers, but her very panic enhanced her loveliness.

Debbie was perfect for the '50s. With her perky wiggle and homogenized blonde face, she could have stepped out of a billboard for the National Dairy Council.

Though we never wrote down a word, Debbie and I spent the summer entertaining one another with *True Confessions* stories. Our favorite was about a woman married to a cab driver with a vasectomy, who gets pregnant by a football player.

OW: Yes, this was the beast that emerged after she was disappointed and hurt.

RH: She doesn't look like a beast there.

OW: Yes she does. Look at that. She looks almost possessed.

RH: That's just because it's an awful picture.

OW: Well, it's still her underneath it.

RH: You've had pictures where you look retarded in them, you can't say that's you underneath it.

OW: I don't know. Yes, that's the veneer over the hurt little Debbie.

RH: What, the beast?

OW: Uh huh. It's like the angel was so hurt by planet Earth that the beast took over.

RH: What I know of you, that's your interpretation of everybody.

OW: I know. It's the human condition.

RH: Yeah, but you're supposed to be talking about Debbie, not the human condition.

OW: Debbie is the human condition.

11. Never act too interested. Make them beg for it.

After the car accident, Debbie couldn't work for a couple of months. She had no money. Otherwise, she never would have stolen the bicycles from Lincoln Park. When her gay boyfriend found out about it, he insisted upon supporting her. Finally, Debbie had attained the status of Kept Woman.

Debbie appeared on the threshold—not at all as he had expected to see her—bewilderingly otherwise, indeed. Her great natural beauty was, if not heightened, rendered more obvious by her attire. She was loosely wrapped in a cashmere dressing gown of gray-white, embroidered in half-mourning tints, and she wore slippers of the same hue. Her neck rose out of a frill of down, and her well remembered cable of blonde hair was partially coiled up in a mass at the back of her head and partly hanging on her shoulder—the evident result of haste.

Writing fiction bores Debbie. She hates description, loses interest in incidental characters. But she loves dialogue. The solution is simple: screenplays.

OW: She projects the image that she just loves to have a good time and she will set up a good time, no matter what.

RH: Yeah, everybody that's with her always has a good time. People she couldn't stand would have a wonderful time when she was there. Don't you wish you had that ability?

A woman named Debbie has always wanted to have a child. She falls in love with a cab driver who has had a vasectomy, marries him anyway, feeling she can do without children, but soon begins to long for them. She doesn't bring up the idea of adoption because she doesn't want to damage his manhood. Or maybe she does bring it up, and he gets defensive about it, and she's afraid to push the point. Nights are long in her empty prefab when her husband drives his cab. She wants to get a job as a waitress, but he forbids it. She takes up hobbies— macramé, painting on velvet. They offer temporary relief, but she drops them after a couple of weeks. One night when her boredom is unbearable, she stops in at the neighborhood bar. Who does she run into but Tad, the captain of the high school football team she was always in love with, but who never paid her any attention. He walks up to her, remarks how she has blossomed. By the end of the evening they have sex. She vows never to do it again and decides not to tell the cab driver because it would break his heart. Of course she gets pregnant. She considers an abortion, but can't go through with it. The cab driver finds out, is heartbroken, leaves her. Now she has a beautiful child, but no man.

After my fiasco with the photographer, Debbie told me to keep away from the arty ones.

RH: What does this show about our relationship? Does it show anything?

OW: No, you might as well be an aunt that she doesn't know in this picture. I see no interaction between the two of you.

RH: Well, we're interacting with the camera.

OW: No. Two different people are interacting with the camera.

RH: But we're posed.

OW: She happens to have her arm around you, but she could have it around a statue.

RH: So, do you think she cared for me?

OW: In this picture, it looks like she couldn't care for anyone.

RH: No, but in real life.

OW: She must have, but it depends on what you mean by caring. You filled a need for her.

RH: Then why would she turn on me?

OW: Because you didn't fill the need for her after a while.

Debbie was delicately lovely, but all ice—glittering, dazzling ice. Still she was alive. Her eyes shone like two bright stars, but there was no rest or peace in them.

Debbie filmed her gay boyfriend staring at her photograph, placing flowers on her grave, remembering her through a dusty picture window.

12. Never let them know how you really feel.

Debbie was friends with this guy who ran a porn shop in New Town. He liked to brag about having opened the first adult bookstore in Nebraska. Supposedly, he used to sell his body through the *Advocate*, but that was hard to imagine with his paunchy belly and balding head. He was as snobbish about drugs as some people are about wine, liked to shoot up MDA. We didn't like one another, but *Witchcraft Through the Ages* was playing at Facets, so Debbie and I stopped by to get some grass. He pulled out an ounce of yellowish marijuana from one of his boots, called it "Marilyn Monroe, the Golden Girl of Dope," and sent us into the back room. Standing there, surrounded by dildos and artificial vaginas, rolling a joint.

> We saw the devil in a movie.
> He had sagging tits, a tail,
> and two horns.
>
> His deformities were
> half female,
> half beast.
>
> The witches lined up
> to kiss his ass,
> and he wagged his tongue
> like any healthy American male.

Debbie lived with a beautiful young gay man who she was violently in love with. He told her he couldn't imagine her as a sexual being, would bring his tricks home, have sex in the living room. Debbie spent a year and a half peeking from her bedroom door, suffering.

Debbie alone beneath her white canopy: the stars don't tinkle, they tick.

> OW: You both were in a similar situation, so it would
> be irrelevant what your personalities would be, in a
> sense, as long as you were at least open to each other.
>
> RH: Well, but if we could talk together all night there
> must have been a lot in common.
>
> OW: I'm sure there was.

Debbie was now, however, inclined to go back to the

apartment and to examine the picture; but the loneliness of the hour and of the place, along with the melancholy silence that reigned around her, conspired with a certain degree of awe, excited by the mystery attending this picture, to prevent her.

Lighting a cigarette in the bathroom, her wet fingers dampening the white paper. This first puff in the morning makes her dizzy and somewhat nauseous, the woman in the mirror with one naked eye, one eye smeared with blue shadow.

Writing this down is an act of adoration.

Two weeks in Chicago. During this visit, I alternated sleeping on the cab driver's couch and crashing with Debbie and her gay boyfriend. Both apartments were in Old Town, so I didn't have to bother with buses. Still, my things were never in the right place, and I was getting tired of using somebody else's toothbrush. I was at the cab driver's when Debbie tried to jump out her bedroom window. Holding a hand to her chest, as if under oath, she told me about her spine. It was driving her crazy. That afternoon she had tried to get herself committed, but a doctor had talked her out of it. This was the first night I slept in her bed.

> RH: If you hadn't heard all the stuff I've told you about her, do you think you would have made these same conclusions from the pictures?

> OW: Actually, I would have been even more cutting.

> RH: I didn't realize you were so catty.

> OW: Well, look at her, you have to be to discuss her.

> RH: She looks like a very attractive woman.

> OW: You see, there's attractiveness, then there's the phoniness, and behind it the hurt little girl.

> RH: Now how do you see that?

OW: Because it's behind every phony, tough as nails woman.

RH: You really know a lot about the psychology of women, huh?

OW: Psychology of human beings.

Debbie didn't get asked to the senior prom. Zipping her skintight blue jeans, she said no matter what she accomplished in her life, it wouldn't make up for that.

I can't remember if it was a Saturday or Sunday, but Debbie's gay boyfriend took me out to breakfast. I felt like a pig, ordering eggs and sausage when all he got was an english muffin. He told me she was a pathological liar. His examples lasted half an hour, but I wasn't interested in his stories, not wanting to be in a position where I couldn't take sides, her side.

OW: She started having her first enemies in grade school. And she also had her good friends, and she turned them against each other. Debbie's enemies and Debbie's friends have nothing to do with each other.

RH: That's true. You know that after she split up with her gay boyfriend, all his friends became her friends and turned against him.

13. Sometimes it's wise to feign anger. It keeps their interest.

Coming from Venus, Chicago's vibrations were too gross for Debbie, so she moved to a suburb. I never saw that apartment, though I can imagine what it looked like.

Before the car accident, Debbie was dying of cancer. Then I never heard about it again, as if the spinal injury had performed a miracle cure.

It didn't matter to me if her stories were true.

Debbie occasionally appears on TV, urging women to purchase a certain diet product, her pleas accompanied by a snapshot of a hundred-and-sixty-pound Debbie. Close-up on the photograph, overdubbed with Debbie's voice intimating disgust a bit too sincere for her role: "See how far I let myself go."

> OW: Okay, now we're trying to reconcile Debbie the hardened woman with Debbie the innocent farmgirl. Even as a farmgirl, you couldn't trust her.
>
> RH: What do you mean, she kicked the pigs?
>
> OW: Because you can see she has an anger.
>
> RH: Where do you see that? She's smiling and looking wholesome.
>
> OW: Look at her eyes. It's in the eyes.

She was only eleven that summer at her aunt's. Her cousin was seventeen. How many times did he tie her up in the barn? Debbie said it made her ass hurt, made her hate men.

The porn shop was only a block from Debbie's apartment. Her friend would drop by on his break or after work, to smoke a joint and shoot the shit. One night they got a real kick out of watching this guy across the courtyard stand naked in his window and jerk off.

14. Decide what kind of man you want and go where he would go. If you want a businessman, go to Rush Street. If you want a poet, hang out at Body Politic. For an artist, take a course at the Art Institute.

Continuity was Debbie's biggest problem in shooting her film. Between the first and second takes the snow on the tombstone melted.

It has something to do with a stripped myelin sheath, a short-circuiting spine. Headaches followed by explosions of light. Debbie focuses all her energy into getting home. Lying in her bed she slowly goes blind, but never loses consciousness as the convulsions begin.

Christmas in Michigan, a welcome break from Chicago. Debbie drives a snowmobile, yelling out, "The sign of the Z!" as she zigzags across the field.

When Debbie was in junior high, her mother made her walk around the house in high heels until she could do it without wobbling.

I felt beautiful, wearing her makeup, her shimmering maroon smock.

After Debbie's affair with the gay man ended, she referred to it as a Palace of Fear. You walk through it, she said, and get colder and colder, slower and slower, until you turn into a blue Ice Princess and are paralyzed. But, you keep on going because the icicles are so beautiful, even as they pierce your heart.

OW: You're secure as long as you're within yourself in that picture, but once you have to interact with the universe, the universe won't play by your rules.

RH: So, you're saying she's the opposite.

OW: Yes, she can play the world of any universe. You could drop her on Alpha Centauri, within ten minutes she'd be dancing with the natives, doing these intricate cultural things.

RH: Could you see how gay men would like her?

OW: Yes. Well, gay men have gone through this too. I mean, deep down, gay men are that little farmgirl Debbie was. They wanted the beautiful romance. Instead, they got beat up in high school, got called rude names, or had to pretend they were one of the boys.

The End

15. Don't sleep with them too soon. Wait until they love you or are willing to pay for it.

He had been out of prison less than a year when Debbie met him. It was at his birthday party. After four black russians they left together, stopping to snort some cocaine on the steps. They spent the night walking along the lake, ended up at her apartment. To him, Debbie was quite a present since he hadn't fucked in seven years.

Debbie kissed his cheeks and they grew rosy. She kissed his eyes and they shone like hers. She kissed his hands and his feet and he became well and strong.

In Debbie's screenplay, a woman with no money sleeps in a graveyard. It is here that all her adventures begin.

Debbie's ex-con boyfriend was adopted at birth, though sometimes he got confused and spoke of childhood incidents with his real brothers and sisters. His adopted parents were wicked and all of his blood relatives, plus his three ex-wives, were dead, many of them dying in violent and bizarre ways. He changed his name every six months because he was Sicilian and wanted to be called Michelangelo.

RH: What do you think of the ex-con?

OW: Actually, look at him, couldn't you see him on Castro?

RH: He would hate that.

OW: I know. You could though. He's one of those older ones.

RH: He looks more like Polk Street than Castro. Or, if he was on Castro, he'd hang out at that donut shop. He doesn't have good taste enough, you know.

OW: He has a body that could, though. He has that tight skin that looks like a lot of people on Castro.

RH: Does this picture give you any new insights?

OW: Just the confirmation that he has no hair on his chest.

Souvenirs of Debbie: a pink wool blanket and hand-blown indigo bowl on a cut crystal stand, gifts from her gay boyfriend. She gave them to me when she knew she was getting married. Also, a maroon-colored satin smock. I wear it as I write this. It doesn't keep my breasts warm.

Never good at lying, I told Debbie I had to work the day of her wedding. She didn't even pretend to believe me.

Debbie told her ex-con boyfriend that her gay boyfriend had constantly been after her body, but she never let him have any.

And never had Debbie appeared more ladylike, in the antique interpretation of the term, than as she issued from the prison. Those who had known her, and had expected to behold her dimmed and obscured by a disastrous cloud, were astonished, and even startled, to perceive how her beauty shone out, and made a halo of the misfortune and ignominy in which she was enveloped.

Force-fed a health food diet for eighteen years, Debbie stocks her cupboard with Wonder Bread and Campbell's soup.

Taking a deep breath and squinting Marilyn Monroe's eyes, Debbie said she let her gay boyfriend crawl into the crevice of her heart, knowing he had the power to destroy her. But, she left him there, not being able to kill the thing she loved.

> you always paint the same woman the
> same woman everywhere
> the woman nude and ravished helpless upon the
> auction block
> hiding her eyes her breasts quiver like moving
> targets

Debbie's ex-con husband had been raped in prison. He swore he would kill her gay boyfriend if he ever met him. I could tell Debbie found this erotic. For the first time in her life, she was having her orgasms in bed.

But Debbie's mortal frame could not endure the exaltation caused by the heavenly visitant, and she was burned to ashes by her wedding gift.

16. Let them feel they're always in charge.

Friday night, cross-legged on Debbie's bed. I had just completed a thirty-page poem. To celebrate, we shared a joint and I began to read my piece out loud:

> The abysmal is aroused
> earth remains earth, sinks down,
> water fills up all the empty
> places.
> Thunder comes
> resounding,
> thus the ancient kings
> make music.

The phone calls began. Debbie smoked instead of answering. She couldn't unplug it because her ex-con could recognize the difference in the ring. He called every ten minutes for the next three hours.

Souvenir. Black lacquer inlaid with abalone, one-legged peacock balancing on a branch of plum blossoms. Inside, a mirror painted with a snow-capped mountain and an irregular blob of yellow and green, suggesting foliage. Two tiny doors with orange-tasseled handles open: a shallow rectangular box lined with indigo velvet. I have filled it with necklaces Debbie has never seen. Winding the key on the bottom results in a most insane rendition of "The Blue Danube," dadadada-da-dada-dada. Another gift from her gay boyfriend.

Debbie's ex-con boyfriend was the first man who liked to cuddle. When he came, his back trembled. Smearing a Q-tip across her eyelid, Debbie told me that when a man's back trembles you have him in your snare.

17.   Men don't like kissing and hugging. They only want to fuck. Quit expecting otherwise.

> RH: Hey, that's Debbie next to him, the pink stripes.
>
> OW: That's a human?
>
> RH: So, it looks like he has his arm around her. What do you think, having seen the pictures of Debbie, of them as a combo?
>
> OW: You'd think that they could really fight. Do they argue?
>
> RH: She told me that she's the one that yells and screams, and he cries sometimes when she yells at him. But, he is very aggressive. Supposedly he was in prison for murdering somebody. He got in a fight and killed them. They had murdered his brother, and he went out and murdered them for revenge. Sounds like he got the idea out of *The Godfather*. Can you imagine her getting together with somebody she even thinks committed murder? From that picture, does she look like somebody who would do that?
>
> OW: Actually, they look like they belong together.
>
> RH: In what way?

OW: They both look like they have very frozen, cold hearts.

RH: Her with her sweet smile looks like she has a frozen cold heart?

OW: But, her sweet smile looks practiced, as I said. They both have this look of contempt in their eyes.

In the dream, visiting Chicago I run across Debbie's ex-con husband. Afraid that he will kill me, I frantically search for ways to sneak past him and see her.

There was a demonic laugh—low, suppressed, and deep— uttered, as it seemed at the very keyhole of Debbie's chamber door. The head of her bed was near the door, and she thought at first the goblin laughter stood at her bedside—or rather, crouched by her pillow: but Debbie rose, looked round, and could see nothing; while, as she still gazed, the unnatural sound was reiterated: and she knew it came from behind the panels. Her first impulse was to rise and fasten the bolt; her next, again to cry out, "Who is there?"

Debbie's biggest fears, besides death, were going insane or becoming a bag lady. She had often felt herself on the edge. "What is it," she would ask me, cigarette trembling, "that gives a person that final nudge?"

For Halloween, Debbie went as a hooker, her ex-con boyfriend a GI.

After she lost weight, Debbie played the lead in *Woman of the Year.* One evening she stopped abruptly in the middle of a scene, forgetting not only her lines, but her life. A nearby observer later reported to have heard her mumble: "Where am I?"

18. Once you marry a man, he's sure to ignore you.

Though I tried to appear indifferent to her ex-con husband,

Debbie knew I disapproved. She had crawled into my brain a long time ago, I could never shut her out.

Books spread across the floor, books on the wall, books crammed into cases as high as his head. The ex-con had finally met a woman with a mind. Debbie was impressed that he read them, indiscriminately. Sitting on the floor, back to a wall, holding Rollo May or Rosemary Rogers, for hours, unmoving, as he did in prison. It made Debbie fidgety just to think about it. And aroused. Her power to make that still body tremble.

Souvenir. Curly blonde girl in a blue cardboard dress with matching bow and anklets, looking pensive. Right index finger touching her cheek, left hand in lap, holding a red rose. Her lips match the rose. An inch and a half behind, her thoughts on a stake: a heart of red roses surrounded by a heart of blue violets, both hearts crossed with a gold key and arrow. Hanging from the violet heart, three more hearts, solid red. White ribbon in the center of the rose heart, embossed with gold: "To My Valentine."

Debbie stayed at the mortuary five weeks, till Christmas. By that time her ankle was thoroughly cured, and her manners were much improved. The mistress visited her often, in the interval, and commenced her plan of reform by trying to raise her self-respect with fine clothes and flattery, which she took to readily, so that, instead of a wild, hatless little savage jumping into the house, and rushing to squeeze us all breathless, there lighted from a handsome black pony a very dignified person, with blonde ringlets falling from the cover of a feathered beaver, and a long cloth habit, which she was obliged to hold up with both hands that she might sail in.

Debbie's loss of memory was temporary, a side effect of chronic jet lag. Doctors prescribed bed rest, but Debbie went on with the play, her role being more important than health.

Standing at the kitchen sink, I think of Debbie, absently consuming an entire jar of marinated artichoke hearts. I haven't bothered with a fork and my fingers are oily.

Debbie had broad shoulders and insignificant breasts. I can't remember ever seeing them naked.

In prison he learned the value of cigarettes. His shirt pocket bulged with two packs. Debbie switched to his brand, and they smoked together constantly, as if each puff were a tribute to their devotion.

19. Don't ever trust a man.

When Debbie's voyeur husband was cheating on her, she would get into her Volkswagen, and, using the psychic abilities she learned on Venus, drive straight to the other woman's front door.

I was moving back to San Francisco, Debbie actually accused me of abandonment. She had grown so distant since her marriage, I hadn't expected this sudden outburst of affection.

Her body was soft and pink and forbidden.

Marrying the ex-con, she felt too mature for Debbie, too modern for Deborah. Her middle name was Dorian, so she started calling herself D.D.

I was back in San Francisco, hadn't found an apartment yet, when the letter arrived. Poorly written and overly dramatic, it came as a total surprise. During the five years of our friendship we had never argued. She called me a "self-centered bitch," warned me not to attempt any further communication. I figured her ex-con husband had demanded me as a sacrifice. Debbie was proving her devotion.

A rose shook in Debbie's blood and shadowed her cheeks. Quick breath parted the petals of her lips. They trembled. Some southern wind of passion swept over her and stirred the dainty folds of her dress. "I love him," she said simply.

> OW: I'm not saying she's an awful person. I'm saying she's coarse.

RH: Well, what would a noncoarse person be?

OW: A shy person. Debbie is not shy from what she projects in these pictures.

RH: No, she's not shy. I've never seen her shy. I mean, I've never seen her act timid. But that was a lot of her thing. She knew how to manipulate and control people, that was like very much her image. Now if I knew all these things—she came right out and told me them, was always saying bad things about her other friends—then why did I just totally adore her and think she was my best friend that I could tell all my secrets to?

OW: Because you thought you were special. It's too bad she's not in Chicago writing a Rosemary piece now.

Grateful acknowledgment made to Hans Christian Andersen, Jane Austen, Charlotte Brontë, Emily Brontë, Thomas Hardy, Nathaniel Hawthorne, Ovid, Ann Radcliffe, Mary Shelley, Oscar Wilde.

White Space

In San Francisco in 1977 I met Linda Betty Myers, a self-proclaimed Southern Woman Writer. Linda Betty had no trace of a Southern accent, but she was working hard to develop one. Her father owned a paper mill in New Orleans—she was raised in a privileged, coddled bubble impenetrable to all traces of regionalism: private schools, therapy since she was born. In her poems, things (such as her little fingers) were often pink and curling like shrimp. I witnessed Linda Betty's first tasting of gumbo—at age twenty-five—instantly she loved gumbo and wore that as a badge of her innate Southern-ness, prominently displayed a jar of filé in her kitchen.

In a pedagogical mood Linda Betty xeroxed me an interview she'd read in which Jayne Anne Phillips spoke of her relatives, who were all dirt poor, of course, how her relatives filled their houses and yards with junk—old tires, empty plastic milk jugs piling up in baroque disarray. The poor Southerners, having nothing, needed all this stuff as a buffer against their emptiness, their despair. Jayne Anne felt that the over-the-top lushness of her writing, all the adjectives and metaphors, her breathless rush of words, paralleled these poor Southern houses swallowed by junk.

I'm reminded of those "garbage houses" the evening news is always reporting being discovered in San Jose or Sacramento. Trash stacked to the ceiling, reek of feces, skeletons of dead animals. I try to imagine the writing of one of their shaggy-headed inhabitants—words jumbled sideways, upsidedown, superimposed—Robert Grenier but more so—a dark indecipherable mass.

For me space and emptiness are intricately linked. For the past six years I've lived in a cramped apartment overflowing with books and files on Jack Spicer. On a bad day I grumble that Jack Spicer gets more cubic feet than I do. I needed this low-rent lifestyle to give me the time to finish *The Letters of Mina Harker*. But I've come to fetishize space, the luxury of walking more than three feet without bumping into something. I once cat-sat for a woman into the simplicity movement. "Buy fewer things, but buy the best—one perfect serving bowl that you can cherish rather than a shelf of bowls you're indifferent to." A monklike stillness permeated Suzanne's apartment, sparse wooden furniture, the gas heater removed, the floors painted white, everything spotless. I'd lie on her cotton duvet petting Ned and reading *Everyday Zen,* all my excess brainstuff dissolving in the clear filtered air. I'd leave determined to turn my life around, to live in peace. But it will never happen— witness the Boschean excesses of *Mina.*

Poets with their line breaks wallowing
in all that white space.

At my father's funeral my brother told me about visiting Grandpa Bellamy in Kentucky, back in the '60s when Joey was in junior high school, and he, Grandpa, was nearing seventy. Grandpa, who was a carpenter, lived in a shack in the woods, no plumbing, dirt floor, unfinished walls lined with newspaper, bare bulb hanging from the ceiling, paranoia, shotgun shells littering the floor like a late Noguchi installation. A simplicity so unZenlike it verges on terror. I've been to Kentucky but once—to see Jethro Tull in a gymnasium—but I'm tempted to seize my Southern roots by the balls, to expand my name to the fullest—Dodie Jane Bellamy. Her prose is so perceptive, so impending, so explosive—she's propped a loaded shotgun at every window.

Spew Forth

Desperate times call for desperate measures. I was eating goat milk ice cream at Veggie Kingdom when I first saw Anya. It was 1979. A petite woman in her early thirties walked from table to table smiling demurely — shoulder-length blonde hair cascaded in soft waves about a pretty, perky face with an upturned nose — she looked like a cross between Michelle Pfeiffer and Lady of *Lady and the Tramp.* "That's Anya," someone said. The most incredible dress floated about her slight frame, layer upon irregular layer of pale blue chiffon, perforated throughout with holes, biggish ones, as if someone or something had once been trapped inside and punched its way out. "That's Anya Steppes," continued the man at the next table. "I love her dress," I said. "It's a replica of the native costume of Venus." "Venus?" I blurted out. He leaned over his soy grit stroganoff. "Yes, Venus — for Anya's a walk-in."

"What's a walk-in? Is that somebody who comes in without a reservation?" He smiled at me with his dark smudged hair, his graphite eyes, infinitely patient. He had an unusually high forehead, like *Eraserhead,* but cute. My hand reached toward him through the bright vegetarian air and our pointer fingers touched with a spark like the fingers of those burly naked gods in that famous, who did it, da Vinci, Michelangelo? "Hi, I'm Carla, Carla Moran." "Yes," he nodded knowingly, "I'm Steven. A walk-in is an enlightened soul who returns to Earth by taking over the body of a lesser soul who no longer wishes to inhabit it. The enlightened soul meets with the unhappy soul on the astral plane and says, 'Hey, I can help you out.' And so the body survives a suicide or a violent accident, then reawakens with the walk-in soul who works to raise the consciousness of mankind. Lots of geniuses and humanitarians through the years were walk-ins — Albert Schweitzer, Benjamin Franklin, Beethoven, the guy who invented the atom bomb. Anya took over the body of a twelve-year-old girl — from Tennessee — who died in a car wreck."

I swallowed the last spoonful of goat milk ice cream, it had a

gamy afterbite like buckwheat or deer, but you got used to it,
"Wow!" "Anya's an advanced soul—*very* advanced—here to
bring the ancient spiritual teaching of Venus to Earth—she's
written a book about it, *One Touch of Venus.*" Later I would
sleep with Steven, later I would hear of Anya dancing on a
table in a leopard-skin bodysuit, cleavage Venusians never
dreamed of, later I would hear how she fucked like a big
blonde cat, clawing and screeching *from Venus she came*—but
that first time in Veggie Kingdom I was so starstuck I dropped
my water glass—CRASH—Anya turned toward me and her
blue dress twirled with her, thin and translucent as dragonfly
wings.

Steven put me on the mailing list of *The Venusian Tattler*, a
newsletter that would keep me abreast of Anya's radio and TV
appearances. "If astronauts landed on Venus," Anya'd tell her
avid or skeptical host, "it would appear empty—save to the
most enlightened—because Venus exists on a higher vibratory
rate than here on Earth. We, the creative, evolved inhabitants of
Venus all have blue eyes and blonde hair. Life on Venus is
more permeable than on your planet—that's why this dress I'm
wearing is full of holes." I learned from Anya that life "on the
physical" is but a phase and therefore thoughts are actions—
and that Jesus Christ was a lower initiate who diluted the
Venusian teachings to match the (lower) consciousness of his
era. On Venus, people could walk through trees or visit
shimmering temples filled with all the great books that ever
have been or ever will be written. Venusians didn't need to
read these books—through osmotic transference their higher
selves were directly linked to the wisdom of the universe. I
placed a copy of *One Touch of Venus* under my pillow—in my
little flat on Valparaiso Street in San Francisco's North Beach—
so that while I slept its secret teachings would drift into my
etheric body and I would understand with a depth that I never
before dreamed possible. The inner Anya knew this, knew that
I was tuned into the higher vibrations of her late-night talk-
radio chatter, knew that I was ready to take the next step. The
following Thursday night, Friday morning, really, I wrapped
myself in my pink chenille bathrobe and switched on my
"portable" Zenith radio, black and chrome it was, mono, built

like a tank. Anya flirted with the DJ as usual. I propped a
pillow against the wall, leaned back in my bed and lit a
cigarette, comforted by her high bell-like giggles. "You're some
far-out chick," the DJ punned. "Rapping with you's like taking
a hit of acid with a sinsemilla chaser!" Anya's voice deepened,
thickened like storm clouds. "Drugs and cigarettes burn holes
in your aura," she declared. "Holes where demons burrow!" I
was smoking two packs of Merits a day and lots of grass and
then there were those mushrooms my roommate brought back
from Mexico and the blotter acid I dropped before the Sarah
Vaughan concert and the MDA I took by mistake . . . my poor
astral body! Punctured and ravaged as a slab of charred swiss
cheese! I felt light-headed, lightened by decay, invisible claws
caressed my throat, invisible lips whispered sinful seductions.
I grabbed the radio for support, its antenna quivered in the
chilly, deathly still air. "Before you know it," continued Anya,
"you're a nymphomaniac food-junkie alcoholic druggy,
feeding the ravenous desires that keep demons clinging to our
planet." Oh no! I took one last drag and threw my cigarette out
the window. It spun like a falling star to the playground below.

I pulled *One Touch of Venus* out from under my pillow and
looked up "demons" in the index. There was a column and a
half of entries! **Demons, auras:** Demons wear binoculars
around their necks to spot new holes in your aura, will use
every trick in the book *money flesh cares of this world persecution*
to get their fix. **Demons, interruptions:** They drizzle sand on
your head as you read inspirational texts, tickle the feet of
babies to make them scream during spiritual lectures
WAAAH! Straight to hell you'll go an elevator, a demon's
blazing finger pushing the buttons. **Demons, language:** The
vilest grunts vomit from their mouths, snarls too obscene to be
translated into English—imagine construction workers'
mouths raised to the highest power—every word in the
demon's lexicon is obscene, as is their grammar, their
punctuation, their dingbats, their typography which is now
your druggy lexicon *your* cigarette grammar *your* punctuation
your dingbats. Every exclamation point is a rape-fuck!!!!!!
Demon-sprache is blotched with underlines italics outline
roman bold, putrid indecipherable swirls and stars—demons

slap their foreheads, bug or scrunch their eyes, point to their temples and stick out their tongues; excretions bubble forth. *MAN OH MAN* @#!!!** HEY **WOW**! Pod-shaped bodies, waddling blobs of emotional cacophony, **"AWK!"** when the Devil chastises one, he clenches the edge of a paragraph, hands and feet poking into the margin, toes crimped under like odious question marks, halo of sweat, jack-o'-lantern mouth ripped open, "GULP OHHH **NOOO** *AIEEEE!*" Arms scrawny and naked as plucked chickens.

I flushed my cigarettes, grass, and diet pills down the toilet and went after Steven like a steamroller. Steven ran the Golden Gate Venusian Study Group, which met every Wednesday evening in the basement of Noe Valley Ministry. A thousand-holed white ceiling, fluorescent lights gleaming across the speckled linoleum floor, dark fiberboard paneling, de-humidifier humming in the corner, a handful of seekers sitting in folding chairs in a circle, eyes closed, chanting the secret Venusian mantra OOOOHH-HOOOOOO-AAIIIIIIIIIIII-EEEEEEEE-AAAHHHHNNNNNNNNN-YYYAAAAAAAHHHH-OOOOHH-HOOOOOO-AAIIIIIIIIIIII-EEEEEEEE-AAAHHHNNNNNNNNN-YYYAAAAAAAHHHH-OOOOHH-HOOOOOO-AAIIIIIIIIIIII-EEEEEEEE-AAAHHHNNNNNNNNN. When we opened our eyes the room looked slightly blurred— brighter, lighter, the air effervescent with spiritual energy. Steven was high-vibed and businesslike, never gave me the time of day. He seemed to favor this other woman, Marsha— Marsha who was always acting so syrupy holy in her puff-sleeved dresses, well I could see right through that holiness of hers, it had more holes in it than the ceiling. Desperate times call for desperate measures—one Wednesday evening I showed up in my seduction outfit: low-slung bell-bottoms that barely covered the crack of my ass and my soft, fuzzy baby blue cardigan. It was tight enough to gape open, with a plunging V-neck. No bra. When I wore this sweater to the food stamp place, the guy gave me a month's worth without even asking to see my ID. I lingered after the meeting as Steven put away the folding chairs, his hair was still darkly smudged, his eyes still graphite. Large, clumsy hands I found endearing.

"Carla, can I help you?" he asked. "Yes," I said, batting my Maybelline eyes. "Steven, it's just that there are certain aspects of the Venusian educational system," dramatic pause, heavy eye contact, "that I just can't grasp." And so it began. His cock was large and his fucking was relentless and cold, it hurt like hell *not HELL!!!* I closed my eyes and imagined I was dying in a blazing plane crash and Steven's cock was a walk-in breaking through the physical barrier. His cum would fill me with glory and enlightenment.

Steven was a Vietnam vet, which I found *way* romantic, all that intensity. He drove for City Cab, but his dream vocation was to sketch tourists' portraits at Fisherman's Wharf. He already had a much-coveted street vendor's license. Once when we were brunching at Zim's he drew me on a napkin, a jagged cartoon woman with vertical slashes for hair, "But it doesn't look like me." Steven's heavy brows furrowed, he reached across his eggs Benedict, took my hand, "It's your inner self." Steven eventually gave up representation—he didn't want to be tied to the physical—and began painting bright biomorphic masses that floated around one another like jigsaw pieces suspended in Jell-O. Depending upon their colors they were called "Life," "Soul," "Etheric," or "Serenity." He also made mobiles, the same blobby shapes cut from cardboard boxes, painted with Day-Glo acrylic, and hung from twisted coat hangers—the air flowing between the forms, he said, was Spirit directing their movements. For our second date he picked me up at 5 a.m. in his cab and we drove to the Bay to watch the sun rise. Steven shuddered, remembering the rats in Vietnam, rats as big as cats *we were souls inhabiting human bodies, we told each other, with enough spiritual discipline we could break the bonds of this plane, visit the wisdom temples, the white deserts of Venus* my heart, like the horizon, turned golden, pink, extravagant.

I had a master's degree, but I was still a child, I'd had sex maybe twenty times with fifteen men, but never a boyfriend. When, after a couple of months, Steven announced he no longer wanted to fuck me, I started crying. I'd always been willing, I even kind of liked it *why why why why why why...* "Steven," I pleaded, "what did I do wrong?" "Nothing, Carla, you did nothing, it's just that after Anya, Earth women just don't do it for me, or not for long, that's all." Anya, Anya, Anya! Long ago she'd moved to Berlin, Anya didn't even send him postcards anymore but he would never move onto me, how bland I must seem how *nothing* beside Anya's Venusian tantra, her extraterrestrial tricks. I sniveled, my lower lip trembling like the San Andreas Fault. He pulled a hanky from his pocket and handed it to me, it was large and white and so soft. "Steven!" I wailed. "Don't worry," he said, taking me in his arms, "there's no reason we still can't sleep together, we just won't fuck, and I'll wear my jockeys." And that's just what we did, sort of. I hated those jockeys, standing between me and his creamy flesh *vile cotton* like Tristan and Isolde's sword. I continued to sleep naked, to spite them. Steven would wait for a perfect moment of unwillingness, when I was asleep or pissed off — the jockeys would vanish and he'd crawl on top, force my legs apart and bang into me so hard my guts sloshed upward squishing my lungs BREATH as he climaxed he yelled out, "WHAT **IS** *HAPPENING...TO ME!!!!*" Then he rolled over and we never talked about it. Once I inadvertently came too, "That was great!" I exclaimed to his back. Steven turned around, his face skewed with disgust, "You treat me like I'm your stud."

Heterosexuality continues to this day to surprise me, the things men present to you as normal *I wondered what was wrong with me that Steven didn't want to fuck me* if a demon bites you teeth marks appear on inaccessible parts of your body, wounds you couldn't possibly have inflicted yourself *white-coated attendants rush in and strap your wrists to the bed, across your chart the shrink scrawls HYSTERIA* on my back, legs open...body-heat bearing down on me, a bellowing boiling cloud, steam tunneled into my cunt scorching clit and lungs, I spread wider *what heaven this brimstone* and moaned, "Steven your thrusts are out of this world." No answer. Then I remembered *Steven's at work and I'm alone in the bed or should be* a body I couldn't see was fucking the shit out of me *the thickness of touch* demon fingers palpated my breasts, indentations dappling across my chest like magic *sparse bristles on back, lines of energy rippling along calves and forearms, hairless armpits, no genitals, demon noses are long as dicks* blow-dryers hidden beneath their nostrils crystallize the moisture in your cunt so that a nose rammed up there chafes and shreds the parched flesh OUCH! When a demon fucks you with its dildo-nose it comes with a big ACHOO *snot for semen* there isn't time for birth control *not a minute* still it took me a full six months to become pregnant.

For we wrestle not against flesh and blood, but against principalities.

After the abortion I started going to a holistic therapist named Donna, a cute woman with shiny brown shoulder-length hair and a chipper smile. She was older than I but still not very old. These are some of the things I never told her about: Steven my fear of being locked in public rest rooms *trapped alive* Anya my terror of falling asleep of turtleneck sweaters of potlucks of salt shakers and sugar jars in restaurants of people on drugs of catching their highs and what if my hands took on a will of their own. My elevator phobia: I would arrive fifteen minutes early, trudge up the six flights to her office, dawdle in the hall until I quit panting. "You look so exotic in those blue earrings," she'd coo. "What adventures has life brought you this week?" "Oh nothing in particular." "*Noth*-ing?" Deeper and deeper did I hunch into the white wicker armchair with its cheerful floral cushion, tainted and abject, my lips a trembling wall of nondisclosure. My eyes traced the arabesques of the oriental rug on the floor. Donna stared at me, her face pleasant and blank until I finally blurted out, "I throw up." "Throw up?" "Yes." "I'm all ears," she chirped. I babbled on about how I was vomiting at least twice a day and it had been over a year—the weight loss was great, I felt intense and sexy, like Joan Jett—but I read about all these women with rotting teeth. She listened, therapeutically silent, then cocked her head and said, "What sign are you?" "Aquarius." Her head shot erect, shiny brown hair jiggling against the lace collar of her blouse, "Yes." Some planet was imminently moving into some house, "So you see," she chimed, "when you're ready to give it up your bulimia will drop away." We decided to focus on something positive. Donna hypnotized me and we found a safe spot on my thigh that I could touch whenever I felt afraid.

The following week she was unusually somber. Her green eyes raced up and down my body like a bar code scanner, then she pointed a finger at me and intoned, "Demonic possession!" She grabbed the silver fairy ball that dangled from her neck on a velvet cord and began rubbing it quickly, the shiny silver ball rolled about between her pert little breasts reflecting the room, reflecting *me* like a third wide-angle eyeball, its tiny clapper tinkling erratically as if the fairy inside were having an epileptic attack. "Vomiting is your soul's way of telling you to get rid of something, only until now you hadn't figured out what." DEMONS!!!! I hadn't smoked cigarettes or done any drugs for nearly nine months, these holes in my astral body, would they ever heal? Silently I chanted *OOOOHH-HOOOOOO-AAIIIIIIIIIIII-EEEEEEE-AAAHHHNNNNNNNNN-YYYAAAAAAAHHHH.* "Have you," I queried timidly, "considered hysteria?" According to Donna, depression and possession go hand in hand—demons crowd your head, causing your brain to swell and press against the skull *like water-weight, like psychic PMS.* "Let's do a little spring cleaning!" I close my eyes and she tells me that my arm is weightless, that helium balloons are lifting it. When my outstretched arm floats in front of me she says, "Demons, can you hear me?" I nod. "Demons, when you died you should have passed quickly to the Other Side, but something went wrong and now you're lost between worlds. I'm here to help you find the way home." Behind my eyelids there is only mottled black, I squint and try to focus these confused beings, whom I imagine to be elongated and wavering. "If you look really hard, you should be able to see a light. Can you see it?" The demons nod. "You don't belong with Carla, you belong with your friends and family who are waiting for you in that light, let go of Carla's aura, walk toward the light. Are they walking?" I nod. "Say goodbye." My floating arm bobs up and down. "Have a nice afterlife, demons. Carla, when I count to ten, you'll be fully conscious and refreshed." But I hadn't seen anything, no lights, no demons, no nothing *I FAILED MY OWN EXORCISM* at home I ate a pint of Chocolate Fudge Swirl and threw it up. As I wiped the sweet acidic froth from my mouth I thought I heard someone or some*thing* mutter *you're going to pay for your big fucking mouth* but when I turned there was nothing, nothing but air.

That night Steven took me to the Royal to see *The Entity*. Invisible forces pummel a female torso, tiny craters dimple across the breasts but it doesn't really look like human flesh, more like the impressions made by your finger when you poke a ball of yeast dough, soft hollows that of their own accord rise back up. But Barbara Hershey is great, so convincing as her body is rhythmically slammed against the bed the couch the wall **AIEEEE AWK!** Scientists trap the demon in a mountain of liquid nitrogen, but it breaks out. Afterward Steven said, "Want to go to Sweet Creations? My treat." "Sure!" As we crossed Polk Street he wrapped his arm around my waist, and I wriggled my hand into the back pocket of his Levi's. From a car radio Phil Collins crooned about something in the air tonight. And he was right, something *was* in the air, a clarity, a heightened charge—I could feel it in the way the concrete sparkled beneath the streetlights, in the aurora borealis of water standing along the curb, in the way the sky sprawled upward and outward forever, a vivid midnight blue. Three-dimensionality seemed to be swelling and stretching like a huge wad of bubble gum, and when it popped a whole new realm would spew forth, a realm filled with harmony and love. The infrared heat of Steven's ass cupping my open palm. Minutes later I spotted the chubby cherubs that frolicked across Sweet Creations' window—damn!!!—I wasn't ready to break free of Steven's body, wanted to curl myself around him even tighter, like a serpent in Eden. We entered the tiny health food bakery, ordered at the counter and took a window seat, the thick sweet scent of honey infusing our hair, our clothes, our words. Steven reached across the table and covered my hand with his large clumsy claw. His electric warmth zapped along my arm and into my cunt *ooohh* I gnawed my leaden sesame cookie and smiled and basked. His dark eyes seemed to glow with new light *intoxicating eyes* a world map spread across the wall behind him, the tip of South America pointing down like a fat finger to the top of his head. "Look, Steven, South America's pointing straight at your crown chakra!" We had a good chuckle over that one. "Barbara Hershey was amazing," I said. "She must have really been molested by demons." Steven sipped his ginseng tea and nodded in agreement. "If any Hollywood star was, it was Barbara Hershey!" He recalled her 1971 rebirth as Barbara Seagull. For one low-budget production she had to kill a seagull on film. It was so freaked out when it died, its spirit flew into her body. "So she took the name Seagull — Barbara Seagull. Like Anya, she's a walk-in! It ruined her career for years. And this movie *The Entity* is her comeback." I squeezed Steven's callused thumb. Maybe tonight was my night for a comeback too.

Steven lived in the Casa Mia, a tidy residency hotel on Columbus near Union. Dorm fridge beneath the sink in the corner, ten-speed leaning against the window, the snores of an old Italian filling the lightwell. As I sat on the edge of the bed taking my shoes off, Steven said, "You told didn't you, you told your therapist about me and you, you told her about the holes in your aura, the *demons* didn't you." I nodded guiltily *how did he know* Steven's high brow collapsed into wrinkles. "I gotta take a piss." I jumped up and grabbed his sleeve. "Wait, Steven, I told her *some* things, but not about you and me." "That's what you think." He shook me off and slammed the door. I went over to the sink for a glass of water, not that I was thirsty, but in the movies they're always offering distressed people water. "Your son's dead, here have a glass of water." As I lift the forest green tumbler to my lips, I hear the sound of horse hooves pounding densely packed Medieval earth, the rattling of windows, willow branches lashing against the panes. A crack opens up in the linoleum, then a golden face emerges with seven glowing green eyes arranged in the shape of a cross, I stoop down and push the middle one, it swirls and steams with molten blood and a pit opens at my feet that extends to the beginning of time and the Earth's hellish core. The colors in the room brighten, glow, swirl, then sag and drip, a glowing blankness, I step around the pit toward the bed, suddenly naked, staring straight into another world where mirrors register monkey heads, my toenails painted blood red. I float downward onto the mattress, gently, the mattress is cold and hard, a marble slab, no dialogue but a thousand fat white candles, their flames lapping the air. Steven enters wearing nothing but his 501s, biceps inflated, he paints ancient symbols on my midriff with a red brush, cold tickle, his face more angular — bestial — than usual as he mounts me and then I see it his giant lizardy eye, I let out a little scream Oh! His carefully manicured claws, two inches long, brush my cheeks, his horns reach skyward, his long ears droop downward straight to hell, the vertical furrows in his brows *up and down up and down* his huge mouthful of teeth his acres of gums, lava red, gleaming with demon cum, it leaks out of all his orifices whenever he's aroused *desperate times* he throws his head back, fucks me slowly and clumsily, his giant wings cumbersome, more jagged than angel wings *my cunt a gash between dimensions* his tail hangs down in the crack of his ass as he humps forward, the marble slab is so cold so hard *love is bruises love is bruises* I only see him in quick cuts, occluded by the sizzling haze of hell but he is truly a marvel to behold, his bubbly luminescent green hide, his sulfurous breath hot as a blowtorch on my flimsy cheeks, his molten red cock, two feet long with a spear-shaped head, there are words inside it, molten words *dreams unwind love's a state of mind* misty psychedelic colors undulate as he brays he loves me in Latin backwards. I am insatiable *my name is Legion* can't get enough of his demon cock *for many demons have dwelled within this body* ripped open by this snorting cloven creature *red face forked tongue* sweating and heaving I come quickly, a fireball of sulfurous farts explodes from between my bloody loins, my screeches break the sound barrier, rattling the tranquil vibes of Venus, booming back I cry out **YIKES!** AIGGEUUUU!!!!

The Mayonnaise Jar

for Sylvia Plath

Sergio was standing next to the stove when I attacked him with the mayonnaise jar. An orange arrow was on the wall behind him, "UNLEADED" printed across it in large black letters. The arrow was pointing down, right at the top of his head. That's where I would have broken the jar if my mother hadn't been visiting from Chicago.

I couldn't bear to make a fifty-year-old woman cry. Ovid tells us that Proserpina was picking wild violets, filling her basket, trying to pick more than any of her friends, when Pluto, great king of hell, spotted her and carried her off to his kingdom on the spot. "With wailing cries the terrified goddess called to her mother, and to her comrades, but more often to her mother."

Sergio is lying in bed beside me. His body feels smooth and cuddly, a naked puppy. I am a beautiful person, he can't express how much he respects me, no matter where he goes or what he does, he will carry around a deep "spiritual" love for me. "Bullshit," I snarl, "I don't want to be loved like a tree or a chair. I want to be loved as a *woman.*" He says he can't do that.

Before the mayonnaise jar, we had been married a year and a half. Then he left.

> For her own sake, Doris should learn to be more tolerant of less capable children. I have certainly enjoyed Doris. I can always depend on her in discussions and she is always ready to take on the extra jobs. She failed to get "Outstanding" only because occasional flares of temper (which she keeps under control) have caused her to do less than her best.
> —L. Levin, 5th Grade

Could I really kill somebody?

Not with a gun or a button, but with my bare hands.

I saw the film version of *The Hunchback of Notre Dame* when I was seven or eight years old. For several nights afterwards my mother had to hold me until I fell asleep. I could handle vampires and giant flying reptiles. Their evil was instinctual, necessary. But this confrontation with human atrocities, especially the scene where molten lead is poured on people, put me in a state of panic.

When he wouldn't leave, the mayonnaise jar was her last resort.

Her father thought it was hilarious when she broke the plastic Kool-Aid pitcher over her brother's head. She was in high school, and Joey, even though three years younger, was already six foot four. It is not surprising, then, that when he came roaring after her, bigger than the refrigerator, she ran into the living room, as if the French Provincial furniture could save her, screaming, "If you touch me, Dad will kill you."

Not with a gun or a button, but with my bare jar.

Sergio didn't defend himself against the mayonnaise jar. Her mother grabbed her hand, his head could have been bloody. He never even flinched, as if he *knew* he wouldn't get hit. In our living room, at the top of an eight-foot wooden pole, a red octagon. Across it in white block letters, a single word: STOP. That night his hands did not find me. He had kidnapped them and was heading for Puerto Rico or Pilsen.

After the Kool-Aid incident, I would hear my mother in the kitchen telling her best friend Stella how she had raised me wrong. A typical Stella response: "Kids are rotten, Winnie." Sometimes a whole week would pass before my mother would remind me to go on a diet. "Don't pay no attention to them."

She sleeps on a foam mat. At the top, where her head goes, the sheet has inched down, revealing a porous manila-colored substance. On the floor, beside the "bed," is a lamp with a glass shade resembling a lily, which would be attractive if it wasn't coated with dust. On the wall, at eye level to a person lying on his or her stomach, are four items attached with pushpins of assorted colors: a magazine cover featuring Toshiro Mifune; a photograph of Bessie Smith; a collage of a naked woman sitting among dinosaurs, the caption "Is it in our genes?" in red letters across her ass; and a white note card with the following lines handwritten in black ink:

> When you put on the skin of a bear,
> you are muscle bone and heart,
> you are grizzle and growl,
> the deadly scent of honey.

When I am alone, the bed gets bigger. Or I get smaller.

The hunchback's love of Gina Lollobrigida made it worse for me. Her beauty next to his deformity—I couldn't bear the contrast. Everything seemed ridiculous and impossible.

> Forty days in the desert,
> a mere vacation.
> The little man inside
> my radiator, nightly banging
> his parched bars. Poor soul
> he may never
> get out.

> Doris is still not using her free time well. An example
> is her Reading Booklet which was a week late. Also
> her social studies project was worked on till the last
> minute. I have had many complaints from various
> teachers concerning Doris' "snippy" remarks and
> attitudes to them. She has shown much disrespect in
> class also—to the children & myself.
> —Carol Dolenar, 6th Grade

She told me that young ladies should keep their legs together, so I slouched down in my desk and spread mine full beaver. No one could believe it when she sent me to the principal's office. Only the dumb kids went there.

The mayonnaise jar had a blue and white label that read "Best."

He had taken his lips off and put them in his pocket. I told him to put them back on and leave.

The only advice my mother gave me about sex was, "If you're with a boy and he starts breathing heavy, go home." She should have been more concerned about *my* breath.

Most evenings while my mother was doing the supper dishes, I would make love with Nance, my best friend who lived down the street. There wasn't a lock on my bedroom door, so my mother always knocked before she entered. Nance and I would inevitably be lying in my twin bed under the covers, and the three of us would pretend we were just trying to keep warm.

On the bathroom door, a study in black and orange:

Peligro!
No Entre.

She was afraid to get up and go pee. What if the Hunchback of Notre Dame was hidden in the shower curtain?

Three weeks later, when Sergio moved back in, neither of us mentioned the mayonnaise jar. I knew if he returned after that incident, he was back to stay. For the first time, Sergio looked at me like a man in love. And the sex is so much better. Most men I slept with have wanted me to come, but never went out of their way to make that happen. Sergio will do anything. Really, I am easy to please. All he has to do is love me like a woman. I never had to tell him how. He already knew.

sliding flesh is so much
softer than
pistons

his
cheek cinnamon and
cloves

loving pumpkin pie
oven
fresh

custard
custard
custard

He claims to be the recipient of instinctual knowledge. When he sits in Golden Gate Park, squirrels climb over his arms and shoulders.

The Kool-Aid pitcher was made of clear frosted plastic which bulged out in the middle. Eyes and mouth were embossed on the bulge, just like the pitcher on the Kool-Aid package. You couldn't buy it in a store. Her mother had to save a certain number of labels and order it direct from Kool-Aid.

When I broke it, the offer had expired. My mother bought Tupperware instead.

Sergio has left me. I am thirty-one years old and crying hysterically on the futon in the spare bedroom. Albert Einstein is above my head, with a famous quotation: "Great spirits have always encountered violent opposition from mediocre minds." My mother, who has not touched me since grade school, is holding me. Before, she was all pillows; now I can feel bone. This display of emotion is embarrassing me, and I am afraid I will feel sexual being so close to her body.

She always knocked before opening my bedroom door.

He told her she was a beautiful person, but he had to follow his dreams, which had left the vicinity some time before the Fourth of July.

My mother pulls me closer when I tell her I am afraid. She says she would like to help me, but she is afraid too.

On the kitchen wall, in black and white and green: "One Chicago. Jane Byrne for Mayor." A cartoon balloon, drawn in blue ballpoint pen, extends from Jane's mouth. Inside it, someone has written: "FUCK YOU MARTY!!!"

My mother told me not to kill him. It was the first time in ten years that she told me not to do something.

Not with a belly button, but with my gun hand.

He says she shouldn't take it personally. He just doesn't want a physical relationship right now. He claims to be the recipient of divine intervention. When he writes he carefully forms all the letters with a clockwise motion because clockwise is holy, and counterclockwise is evil. He says government agents trail him in semicompact cars. He says I should wear gold instead of silver because gold is more spiritual.

I don't remember why I broke the Kool-Aid pitcher over his head. Consequently, the action has an amputated quality about it, floating around in my memory with a logic of its own which has transcended any sibling squabbles. He did used to call me "queer," and I would act all shocked and offended. Maybe that had something to do with it?

Sergio is standing next to the stove when she attacks him with the mayonnaise jar. An orange arrow is on the wall behind him, "UNLEADED" printed across it in large black letters. The arrow is pointing down, right at the top of his head. That's where she will break the jar if her mother isn't visiting from Chicago.

> Doris is a very pleasant child and a good worker. She tends, at times, to become very bossy which I have tried to talk to her about. She has improved some and I am sure she will continue to do so.
> —Myrna Nickelson, 2nd Grade

I am in bed with Marsha, a woman from my writing workshop. We are naked and curled around one another at the waist, like two links of a chain. It feels intimate and sensual, but not sexual. I tell her I wish I could touch all my women friends like this. In class the next day, I decide not to mention the dream. Strangely enough, Bob, our instructor, jokes that Marsha and I should become lovers so we could get published in lesbian magazines. "No," she replies, a bit too quickly. "We are both too good in bed. We would be competing with one another." I almost blurt out, "I used to be good, but not anymore." Thank god, I don't, but then I wonder why I would want to say such a strange thing.

Do I really want to touch my women friends? After a couple of times of me stiffening, they usually quit trying to hug me. Evangeline and I used to hold hands during another writing workshop. Though warm and innocent, it felt scandalous enough to be exciting. Once, when parked in her Volkswagen, which always smells of gasoline, she hinted for me to kiss her on the mouth. I told her I didn't want to get involved with a married woman. We both knew we were supposed to laugh, and so we did. I can't remember if I wanted to or not.

When the bed gets bigger, I get smaller. Or, alone.

During college vacations, I would tell her she had been a good mother, but she never seemed convinced. I was a Phi Beta Kappa, I would remind her. Really, she hadn't done that bad.

No one in my family, including myself, had ever heard of Phi Beta Kappa until I was nominated for it. My mother's favorite course in high school was filing, her favorite books are psychic murder mysteries. I read one. It was about a woman who had a cornea implant, which was successful except that the cornea originally belonged to a murder victim, and the woman kept having visions of the hypodermic needle used to administer the dead woman's drug overdose. I was captivated. My father quit school after the seventh grade. He would sit in his green plastic armchair and brag about having read Kipling's *The Jungle Book.* It is the only book he has ever read.

I was too embarrassed to tell my friends I got good grades, not wanting to appear straight. A person was "straight" when he or she had any interests other than getting fucked up and listening to the Allman Brothers.

In college she was very lonely.

> Doris does very creative artwork and makes good use of her free time in worthwhile learning activities. She is occasionally critical of the other children; sometimes it makes us happier just to accept others as they are.
> —E. Ravenscroft, 1st Grade

> Tell me that you love me.
> Tell me that you love me.
> Tell me that.

Often my mother would assure me, "Don't feel you have to tell me everything. What I don't know don't hurt me." She would say this as if she was certain that just about everything I did out of her sight would hurt her.

My bedroom door would always knock.

On the closet door, two royal blue life-size footprints in a field of smudged white. Between the feet, also in blue, a guarantee:

> OUR AUTO MAT SERVICE
> "We Kept It Clean
> While We
> Worked On
> Your Car."

Sergio hopes they can remain friends. She says she already has plenty of "friends." When he was leaving, the mayonnaise jar was my last resort.

My mother has never questioned the men I have chosen, even though a number of them have been highly questionable. I suspect she would be content with the Hunchback of Notre Dame, just as long as my lover is male.

I can't remember if I wanted to or not.

He has a scar on his ass from when he fell onto a dolly at work. I rub it and put my lips real close to his ear, whisper, "I like a man with a scar." Sometimes I call him Humphrey Bogart.

Her father, a carpenter for the public schools, wears her Phi Beta Kappa key to work. In the boiler room, he shows it to the coaches he is playing poker with. "Straight *A*s," he says, taking a drag from his unfiltered cigarette.

The woman in the bathroom mirror looks tired, but attractive. She is closer to Lollobrigida than usual. If a man were to enter, she would hunch over and gnarl like the exposed root of a tree.

My mother often complained that she had wasted her life, spending thirty years in a green shingled house, vacuuming the carpet and cooking dinner. I would try to comfort her, saying, "Mom, the way you were raised, you had no choice." Still, she had always dreamed of being a secretary. If she could live her life over again, that's what she would do. After spending two weeks in my life, she flew back home looking forward to seeing my father and the vegetable garden. I didn't hear from her again for six months.

Reptilicus
(with Kevin Killian)

"at midnight, when the moon makes blue
lizard scales of roof shingles and simple
folk are bedded deep in eiderdown..."
—Sylvia Plath

Extinct Species

"Jane Doe," said the announcer on TV, "a woman famous for forgetting. Over a quarter of a century of memories erased from her cramped gray matter." Next morning I saw another account in the *Chicago Sun-Times*. "Global amnesia, forgetting a world or a world forgetting?" For no one knew who she was, this woman found buried in a Florida swamp, who ate flies and beetles and who had developed a rudimentary tail like an alligator. She'd been dug up out of the mud by mystified contractors. They showed her on *Nightline,* nodding and grinning and hissing, while I munched popcorn in my den.

On the screen her moving, puzzled face looked oddly familiar, but the stiff newspaper photo was that of a stranger. I shook my head and turned the page, sighing for the homeless. And especially for "Jane Doe." Funny that I had once known a woman named Jane, but was there a resemblance? What would it be like, I thought later, to have forgotten everything, every sense, every memory, every knowledge? Gone the greasy bobby pins pinched between front teeth, gone the bitter aftertaste of cottage cheese and saccharin, the dark biting sweetness of chocolate-covered cherries behind a locked bedroom door?

Gone the six-foot stubble-chinned carpenter who hammers between my sheets, the milky curve of my breast, his noisy suckle?

Gone the patent leather thrill of stepping on every crack, gone all my childhood?

Gone the crotch itchy with perfumed aerosol powders, my cunt sucked dry from cotton plugs, gone the fat winged vulva, thighs clenched to clamp its untimely flutters? And nineteen years of gooey anticipation for that first five-minute back-seat fuck. Well, was it worth it? Again I uncrumpled the *Sun-Times* page. "Global amnesia, a ten-megaton neural explosion, the past wiped off the face of the mind. Psychiatric nurses admire her 'infinite potential.'" Well, I could imagine! A woman with nothing but a blank pained stare, a twitch, part of a tail! Who knows what twisted imprints await her in subterranean strata, what three-eyed mutant watches from beneath the wavy black edge of sanity?

Socio-Economic Background

The Jane I grew up with in Oak Park always wore a push-up bra, and her favorite book was *Gone With the Wind*. I liked *Catcher in the Rye*. She had the same perky nose as her mother. We used to argue over *Route 66*, I preferred the dark sleazy George Maharis, Jane the bland blond brotherly type, Martin Milner. While I sat at home studying Baudelaire, Jane started dating a boy named Chip, who always could get his father's Capri.

"We live in a misogynist, patriarchal society," I'd tell her, and she'd look at me blankly, her eyes glazing. "I don't know what you're talking about." "Well, look it up in your Funk & Wagnalls." "I never read the dictionary," she said, with an arid glance. "Reminds me of foreigners in high school history."

In school she sat next to me, her ballpoint pen idly bluing the FUCK carved into her desktop.

How now, Jane? In Chicago her logical conclusion would be to wind up one of those old women at the front of the bus, impeccable in a pink linen suit, thighs open like a yawn, meshed dark of nylon tops peeking out two inches above her knees: this breach but a temporary lapse in etiquette, one of those moments in every woman's life when it is difficult to remember to be a lady from the waist down.

Chicago —

Metropolitan mafia ghetto, hard-working hog butchers, an unending loop of truck drivers murdered in gas stations in the middle of the afternoon, women raped on el platforms at rush hour. But Jane and I commuted from a northern suburb. No one got knifed in our maple-lined neighborhood with its Frank Lloyd Wright houses.

Later I learned the tricks of sidewalk survival, to lock my purse under an armpit, ready for the shadowy assailant, keys clenched in fist, ready to spear his blood red eye. But I doubt Jane ever had to.

Lake Michigan misting the atmosphere, invisible with night and distance. Before dawn Jane would float to work in her Volkswagen bulb, savoring the chocolate dark comfort beneath its shiny red shell.

She was its brain on a highway of beacons. Her headlights bounced off the green exit sign, its silver studded border glowing through her windshield. I sat beside her in the next seat breathless with feminism, babbling theory and watching her profile.

Her desk — six square feet of personally organized territory, buzzing shadowless fluorescence bleaching her already pale fingers. Mechanical blur of knuckles melting into her IBM Selectric's ivory keys. I found her hypnotic and you would have, too.

Who would ever think she'd change? When she moved to Florida with her new boyfriend Michael, I followed her there, too. At least for my two-week vacation. Called up and invited myself to stay. "Sure, why not?' she said carelessly, long-distance wires trailing through the night. We had a bad connection, did she really say, "Surely not"? I couldn't decide, all the way down in the plane till I saw her face at the airport, in the heat of the Florida night.

Jane Heads South

Something was inching down my back—sweat? It woke me.

Not sweat, but the flutter of shiny brown feet: a flying palm roach the size of a mouse.

"That's Florida for you," said the boyfriend, who came into my room when I screamed. "Where people go to retire." Why hadn't *she* come?

Outside her window bamboo clattered, walking wooden ghosts. From banyan branches hung elegant spotted orchids, their plastic Martian beauty reminding me how far I'd come from Oak Park. Florida is a paradise of parasites. The bungalow was built on shifting sands, under the floorboards I heard swamp life flutter and ooze, the earth shifting in gritty protest.

Jane no longer did office work; instead she worked as a bike messenger. She'd always been good behind the wheel. Her lover lived on disability because he tried to commit suicide in the Navy. He was a dark snoring hulk in a hammock. Jane's lips were salty with ocean, when she met me at the airport gate. And she kissed me.

We drove around some, and she pointed out the love bugs— "just like me and Michael"—that fuck in midair, fuck themselves to death on the highway, their ecstasy spattered all over her windshield. I asked Jane what it was like having a boyfriend who lies around the house all day. Her sunglasses tipped down her nose. Her eyes were green as key limes. "He lets me be me," she said. "Sure, I take care of him, but he lets me be me."

Jane had built a shoulder-high pyramid of Mountain Dew cans against one of the stucco living room walls. My first morning there I cracked my bedroom door and peeked out: Jane was sitting pretzel-legged before her pop altar, wearing nothing but latex biking shorts. As I tiptoed toward the bathroom I saw that her eyes were closed and she was holding something in her lap—a jar of flies that were buzzing furiously—then Jane began to hum to them and the flies calmed down, silently speckling the glass like blemishes rather than living creatures.

At the time I didn't think that much of this—Jane had never had much of a flair for interior decoration—and they say on *Dick Cavett* that meditation is good for you. But on the plane home I wondered how deeply she'd gone under, her swamp a sweltering hole so black she could sprout a tail, and Michael would never even notice. He'd just let her be her.

Beneath her sticky epidermis, scales were shifting, itching to pop out.

Out of Wedlock

"Why don't you get married?" her mother wrote. "Because," Jane thought, "I'm an individual." She might as well have been a Mrs.—one man, one bed, sheets that stink in less than a week.

On Jane Doe's left hand, the papers say, nurses found a wedding band engraved with a date eight years old. The patient cannot refute the tally. Her therapists have yet to teach her to remember her love life. If any.

Belching his Bud and puffing a Salem, Michael warned Jane about the grocery, the laundromat. To listen to him, you'd think men were waiting to rape her with a stalk of celery, to tear at her cotton shift, blue flakes of detergent caked beneath their nails. "What are you, my keeper?" she snapped.

She dumped her pantyhose down the incinerator, even the ones still packaged in plastic eggs. Tattered or unhatched, they all melted in that basement inferno; Jane's legs grew thick and hairy. One of her letters, that I re-read the other night, asked me if I thought this might mean she was a lesbian. She shed her secretary figure for a man's shirt, lumps of breast and ass bagged in blue flannel undulations.

Strange desires began to visit her in the night, she wrote, but she didn't specify what they were. The sudden urge to ambush bugs with her tongue? Shit in sand? Hook her knees over a branch and hang there, like her beautiful orchids, to hang upside down until gravity sucked the mental relics right through the top of her skull? Yeah maybe! I mean the more I look at these pictures I seem to be seeing the same girl.

Sex with Michael was never unpleasant. It gave her time to think, and she had much to think about. Washing out her panties in Woolite, movies with black horses, the inevitability of coffee. And when he came, his breath was a tornado whirlpooling her back to a greener era where she would never sprawl like this, her unshielded belly reflecting the moon.

Eventually we, her friends in Chicago, began to ask too many questions, and she stopped corresponding—with any of us, as far as I know. Neighbors' gossip seeped in through the windows like poisonous gases. She got Michael to board over those gawking glass eyes.

Jane bowed her head, shifting her twinging vertebrae. Mutable, silent marrow, she settled into the plasterboard cave.

She had a sixty-watt lamp, of course, at the flick of her finger, but Jane preferred the eternal night, the fossil-faint outline of a table, blurred curve of an unmade bed.

The blackout was not void, but a growing vortex of breath. Visions filtered through cracks: delicate feather plants, weightless as souls, shadow and leaf merge, green air, green dew, quivering exhalation of green light.

Faint buzzing of bees in left ear, she greeted the walls with a honeyed tongue.

Love Sonnet

I came back from Florida with a tan everyone envied, and a coral necklace. When her letters stopped I wasn't exactly surprised. Maybe Michael had told her I'd let him sleep with me. Once. Once or twice. But he'd told me she didn't care what he did. His cheekbones dissolved, I crawled into his brain, a warm blanket world. In the sand between his toes I burrowed and wriggled. I curled in the crack of his ass like a thong bikini. Then I swiveled him around like a lazy Susan and caught Jane's yeast infection.

Can you blame me, Jane? His basking granite back drove me insane—I blurred to a drop of protoplasm sinking through strata of itchy knowledge, your knowledge. *Jane,* I wrote, *this silence is like a wall between us, don't harden your heart to me, I shed stone soup tears.*

Laundry

STOP: Dryer Is Hot. Padded bras, baby pants, foam rubber, nylons may burn or melt. WATCH CAREFULLY.

Okay. Black porcelain hatch, black as Jane's bedroom, hotter than the Sunshine State they found Jane Doe panting in. Black hatch a 25-cent death chamber for children and small animals. Every time I do laundry I can't help but think of that poor poodle in the *Enquirer*.

Steaming terry cloth swirl, fabric softener sickly sweet as gardenias. I toss in my sex. Okay. Scorching silver globes of blue jean studs brand my shrinking vulva. Smoldering neurons deaden to pain. It gets so numb in the laundry. I leave for a while then come back when the cycle is done.

Wide arc of furnace porthole, opening. I lean in, and I feel a little like the witch in "Hansel and Gretel," and a little like Gretel herself.

I remove the pink ash. With a single stamp I could slip it in an envelope, ship it back to my mother. It would fall into her palm, a crumbling wisp of tissue, no bigger than the umbilical scab.

Night in Captivity

Outside the bungalow Jane heard snakes and lizards, heard them inching in. Inside, a plaster collision. Her head banged the wall three times before arrest. She was alone in the room. *Did I do that?* she thought. *Am I trying to punish myself?*

Purple blossomed beneath her forehead, a painful plum. The sugar bowl shattered. She watched her hand spout shards of glass. *Punish?* No use tossing the crystals over her shoulder: anything resembling dandruff was socially unacceptable.

Wooden slats surrounded her, dusty horizontals flat as a shadow, but stiffer. Clothes creased and wrinkled, stepped on, or over. Whiff of black bowels too weighty to be swept away.

The screen door slams. Michael drives away with his duffel bag full. "You need Dr. Joyce Brothers. I'm out of here."

Bodily emissions ooze and drool...sheets that need Kleenex and a grandmother   dumb rub   of dead sex

only the living wail. Why won't he believe her when she tells him she is not a woman, she is a genie   his hard fuck will never release her.

Where is the humor in a bruise? This airtight bleeding so dark, so dark. One slit of oxygen would brighten the effect.

A Piece of Cake

Black forest. Chocolate dark layers, earth cake. Cherry pink whipped cream, blood mixed with snow, melts in my belly, a slow boil. Mud-thick icing, slivered almond scales.

A gooey communion: coffee and this subterranean sweet body.

I know it's true. I read it in Science Digest:

In 1551 a Brazilian tribeswoman ate her French lover's neck. Slowly chewing she savored each pink mouthful. Soon afterward, she developed a craving for chocolate mousse and Rabelais.

The female of a certain species of frog swallows her own eggs. But her digestive acids are merciful: weeks later, a fury of green birth heaves from her gaping, hysterical mouth.

Any beast's body is directly proportional to her oral consumption, I read it in *Science Digest*. A change in what she stomachs equals an amendment to her genetic constitution.

Jane and I used to laugh at the crazies, the way they flock to Dunkin' Donuts. One day our tweed-suited boss began to growl at her luncheon salad. "I'm sick and tired of rabbit food," she said with a quick scream, and pushed it aside and scurried to the bakery, with us in tow like two little avatars of curiosity, it's always so encouraging when someone you know goes off the deep end. At the counter she wolfed down *bags* of fat-forming goodies, oblivious to us and to the gathering crowd. She didn't even think to vomit them away. That night Jane phoned. "Next time you see *her,* she'll be a bag lady on the park bench with one of those Styrofoam platters of spoiled shrim—" "—scooping them up with her fingers, little pink crescents speckling the sidewalk,—" "—ketchup smeared across her gnawing jaw, like the blood they use in monster movies."

But think about it: what's really in corned beef hash, or in that can of SpaghettiOs? You never know what those Spanish ladies stuff inside their burritos. You *think* you're eating chicken, but could you recognize the taste of lizard tail entomatado? Read the Food section of the *Sun-Times:* "Genetically, those vertebral tidbits are the state of the art, programmed to snap off easy as an asparagus stalk."

To regenerate in subterranean humors.

You never know when a woman will crack, never know what dark scales swell inside your own skull, what sort of egg tooth is chipping away at your porcelain complexion. The heart beating its thick red fever, you never know what is in there, feeding.

Volcanic bowel eruptions, what black biles fester in those aging tissues?

The fire of decomposing matter can hatch an egg. Is that a birth cry, that hoarse rattle beneath your heavy breathing? In the beginning the world was but a dimple on the divine serpent's belly. That dimple, that sudden burst of animal magnetism, those tremors in the hypochondrium, could they be the thrashings of half-formed claws?

Bedding the Bog

It was the mud between her toes that pulled her back. She lay down, sister to microbes and salamanders...in the thick mud of Florida, tropical chocolate   thick ebony yolk.

Swallowed by mud a soft sideless indifference. She could sink a million years and never reach bottom. Neither dark nor light, this part's like an Operation Rescue film on the eyeless silence of the unborn, total cellular suckle.

Gravity releases her original molecular buoyancy. She is solar inside.

Protoplasmic spores ferment and swell, fingertips touch Mars...toes roll over Uranus. *Mud!* Mud that sucked that last warm-blooded memory from her marrow; that ate a tunnel through the flimsy tissue of this life. Ate past fur and milk and bloody thighs; ate past arrowhead and fossil; ate to steaming breath thick with volcanic ash, to massive claws encrusted with crushed ferns, centuries of dead skin shedding. *AVE REPTILICUS!*

Mud sucked at her flaking dermis, back and legs beaded pink, prismatic circulation of jeweled scales, asbestos and lava fuming between her thighs. Mud venom dilates the nether eye. The great world egg is ready to be laid.

And the mud sucked cartilage ions into a tail; flex of back and ass, whooshing vertebral waves, streamlined elongation of snout, an arena of delicate ivory blades inside. Three-chambered coronary fusion. Vertical slits in pupils: night vision intensifies. *Reptilicus!*

Blind spot before her, microscopic universes swell in the periphery.

Bubble gum stretch of tongue tripled in distance—she can flick it like a whip, lick up a thousand shiny brown bodies. She opens her throat wanting to sing but the only thing the soundtrack picks up are your standard haunting growls, croaks, snorts and snarls like an old Patti Smith album. Every beast and vegetable loses its name

> pristine vibrations
> mud quakes and shimmers
> a sea of velvet echoes.

Chicago Bus

Bulging plastic garbage bag tenderly pressed to bosom, blue and green housedress stolen from Goodwill bin at midnight, bare-breasted undulations, ocean and fern, a bag lady hobbles aboard the bus. Her feet are cramped into shredded white tennis shoes—ridiculous straitjackets for the tough agility of toes genetically perfected through millions of years of climbing. I see her every day. It's like she's on my schedule.

There's a brown suit at the steering wheel. Absently she shows him the crumpled transfer foraged from the gutter. In her armpits fester dark organisms, swamp fumes seeping down aisle, nylon-legged ladies cover their noses. I try not to cover mine, but I just can't help it. She plops beside a window, in a plastic orange seat, patch of sun to bask in.

Soiled gray overcoat wrapped around her, bag cuddled tight against body like a plump child, she unties its wrinkled polyethylene neck, stuffs in the transfer, memories traded for wadded bits of rubbish and newspaper. She spreads her thighs like a fan, flesh gritty with volcanic ash.

Oh, Christ, would you *look at her tongue?* Vibrato siren of housefly, winged blur at safety glass, reflex spring action of tongue, she locks her jaw to stop herself, adhesive bulb at tip battering the back of her teeth.

Her iridescent tail, her parched hide peeling in large transparent flakes,

bonechilling dreams electrified,

the night a galaxy of dark products, in any one of them this unwomanly woman's glowing red eye.

Her ancestors were giants, quaking sun-baked clay, fangs big as elephant tusks, fire-breathing oracles loping through forests at fifty miles an hour, furious green trembling with every leap. She has no respect for us, the other passengers on the bus. These night-blind mammals with their beady stares, descended from the flea-bitten shrews that cowered before the Ancients' mighty claw.

It's like global amnesia is *global, no one* remembers.

If the Jane Doe in the papers is my Jane, how could Michael have deserted her? Once recovered, perhaps she should find a zookeeper, fall in love. Life would be easy behind his bars, every day the same rock to crawl under, every night a scientifically balanced diet. Occasionally he would slip his hand through one of the open verticals, lovingly fondle her bumpy forehead. Weekly a thousand human eyes would marvel at her every movement. *No need to fear,* the cage walls and sign would assure them: *she is a separate species, exotic, a bit bizarre, yet officially uncontagious.*

The bus bumps on; I keep my watch. The way her toenails curl beneath her feet, and that ragged overcoat. Why in this suffocating heat does she hide beneath it? What is this flaking of skin at wrists, that damp reptilian odor seeping from sleeves?

Across the aisle, poster of a woman, puffy hair, shiny pink mouth, tiny gold globes on earlobes. Black letters printed across the woman's neck, I watch my bag lady stare at them, uncomprehending: "Rosalyn Snitow/Victima de Hemorroides." Slowly she fingers the greasy wool of her overcoat, opens her cracked lips. I am reminded of someone I might have known.

Dear Diary Today

Could Ken imagine himself sleeping with a woman? His answer: Could you imagine yourself fucking your cat? Lying in his bed, watching the news, he keeps leaning against me. He's fluish, so I figure it's delirium or he wants a mother's attentions. I slug his arm and say, "Get your disgusting body away from me." He laughs, but doesn't move.

Sergio lies in Ken's bed too, sometimes in the middle, and we both lean against him. More often, I am in the middle with Sergio on the outside and Ken by the stereo. We eat cookies and popcorn, crumbs gritting the sheets. These moments are good as a hot bath.

Yesterday a man came over for lunch. I fed him tuna salad on sourdough and warm beer, and he fed me accusations: I was taking things too fast, I was trying to define our "relationship." Pouring boiling water over coffee, I said words like "ridiculous" and "absurd." Since we don't fuck I thought things between us would be easy.

A woman behind me on the stairs, panting. She says, "My cardiovascular system can't take this."

Becoming a Heroine on the subway, approaching the Montgomery Street station, I underline: "Gossip, like novels, is a way to turning life into story. Good gossip approximates art; criticism of novels is mostly gossip." In the periphery, fluorescent lights and yellow.

I feel guilty when I gossip, but what if I change the names. Instead of Ken, read Oscar, instead of Sergio, Fire Hose, instead of me, you. And that was a woman at my kitchen table. She has red hair and smokes Gauloises, her secret vice is a passion for Bananarama.

Sergio wants to buy a rainbow filter for his camera so that every scene can hold one. I imagine a headshot, my crooked smile, rainbow gleaming across my forehead. Walking along Dolores Street, he puts his arm around my shoulder and whispers, "Let's find some bushes."

A says B is moving to San Francisco from Chicago, but don't tell C because A wants B for a roommate. C, who was laid off, is spending his unemployment checks in leather bars. D is shocked. E's ex-husband, F, who lives in Nebraska, is calling and writing to G in Indianapolis. G's twin sister, H, is living in Denver and has just left her husband. I's catering business in Palm Springs has fallen apart, so he will soon be moving to San Francisco, as will J, whose contract in Japan is over. And E's new lover's name is K.

He sat at my kitchen table for six and a half hours. I yawned and he still sat there. Then we said goodbye and I thought how could somebody sit at my table for six and a half hours and me not know if they had a good time.

So I lie in Ken's bed and tell him how I felt. He shows me his latest computer program: WELCOME TO THE MAGIC RECIPE SHOW. THE FIRST THING WE ARE GOING TO DO IS RUN THE ENTIRE LIST OF FOUR (4) RECIPES PAST YOU, JUST TO IMPRESS YOU.

>AGED EGGS
>SHATTERED DREAM BRITTLE
>AMBROSIA OF THE GODS
>PAST LIFE STEW

I'm tired of fiction, you can be my journal. I got up this morning and brushed my teeth, thinking of a dentist. Lizzie says I gossip because my moon is in Gemini, as is hers and the man at my kitchen table's.

AGED EGGS. PLACE EGGS IN TIME CAPSULE FOR 200 YEARS AND THEN PREPARE AT WHIM.

The front of the bus, two women across from me, obviously mother and daughter. The mother wears lime green knit pants, the daughter a matching lime green knit jacket. I am touched by this evidence of sharing, try to imagine the daughter with her mother's legs and vice versa.

Sergio and Evangeline like each other. That's because their sun and moon are reversed.

If my kitchen table were Ken's bed, would the man sitting there be a cat?

In her new poem, "Remoteness," Marsha writes that white Toyotas frighten her. I went thought the same thing with red motorcycles. Anything could happen. Sergio could leave me. The Bank of America where Ken works could be bombed. Or I could have an affair with Marsha.

A Leo and two Aquarians sat in the Leo's bed. All three were from the Midwest. This was the position of the moons: Virgo was on the outside, Aquarius was next to the stereo, with Gemini in the middle. When Sergio's not around we take cold pills and zone out on Penderecki and Boulez. Ken makes flash cards of pictures of modernist composers and flashes them at me. "Webern?" I say. "No, Shostakovich."

I sit down, choosing a seat where no one in my direct line of vision appears crazy or likely to attempt eye contact. Half a carnitas tostada fills me, but I keep eating to get my money's worth. Through the window I see a white Toyota parking on 17th Street, but I'm not frightened, just nosy. The driver's door opens—no, it's not Michael, so I turn my attention to the woman at the next table, probably in her 50s, who opens a compact and a tube of fuck-me red lipstick, which she slashes her cheeks with. Then she rubs her red-slashed cheeks in a circular motion, finishing them off with little upward strokes. She looks like a clown, the tips of her fingers a cherry blur. It's too crowded for me to refuse him, so a man sits at my table. Fuck, an eye contactor. Not even cute, slimy. I avert his gaze and pull on a thick black sweater to cover my breasts. I'd leave, but there's half a bottle of Dos Equis to go. Being the only woman in my building I get to blame every minor agitation on men. Tomorrow morning men will blast disco music at 9:30

and use up all the hot water, so I have to take a cold sponge bath. A man is making me gulp my Dos Equis when I want to linger on the woman with the ruby cheeks. Gulped beer makes me dizzy.

SHATTERED DREAM BRITTLE. MIX SHATTERED DREAMS WITH EXPERIENCE AND BAKE WITH REGRET.

Two lesbians sit on my left, two gay men on my right. A table on either side separates me from both couples. I spread my thighs and drink Dos Equis, trying to pull off Independent Woman. Sergio and I haven't had sex for two days, but we will tomorrow at 5:30 and it will be good as a fantasy.

Last weekend Michael of the white Toyota slept with a new woman. A couple of days later at Marsha's reading, when I mentioned his latest conquest Michael was impressed with my connections and gave me the details. I slept with him myself six months ago, but swore to Sergio that I didn't. He has the largest cock I've ever seen, but was kind of cold. Marsha *should* be afraid of him. At her reading I also heard something about the man at my kitchen table that surprises even me. But I won't tell you about it, not wanting anyone to think I can't keep a secret.

AMBROSIA OF THE GODS. MIX AIR FREELY WITH NEGATIVE IONS AND INGEST EXCLUSIVELY FOR 20 YEARS.

I wiped tuna fish crumbs from the formica counter. We're friends, I told him, it's an indefinable relationship. He sat there silently, with a skeptical look on his face, arranging little plastic animals on my kitchen table, and I wished he were my father so that I could go to my room and slam the door. In the background Messiaen's "Quartet for the End of Time" struggled on toward beauty. Why does everything reduce down to sex with me, I'm not even attracted to him, he's got to be forty and he's so skinny. I suppose that words equal sex, or at least enough words, six and a half hours' worth.

Ken says I can have any feelings I want as long as he's not

expected to respond to them. Every white space is a censored urge. Tomorrow Evangeline will not be going to Europe, but she will have written a piece in which she copies the form I stole from Marsha who got it from Kathy Acker. A high school boy on the corner, breaking a bottle. He says, "Now somebody will step on it and cut their foot." His friend laughs, adding, "I'm all for that."

Yesterday a man was coming to lunch, so I cleaned my apartment except the bedroom because I knew he wouldn't be going in there. The puddles of dirty clothes on the floor are friendly, I lie down, having taken off everything but my purple T-shirt and lavender underpants. The underpants are ripped in front, as if someone has slashed them with a knife. My pubic hair shows through, it is red, and I play with it, absently, like a person clicking a ballpoint.

As we lay in his bed—the man at my kitchen table's, not Ken's—he read me Robin Blaser's "The Moth Poem," talk about mixed messages.

I fall asleep with the light on, my bed scattered with books and pens. Sergio wakes me around five, complaining about electricity and how's he supposed to get beneath the covers with all this crap in the bed. Picking up my things he says, "Why are you sleeping with the lights on?" I mumble groggily, "To keep away the ghosts." "What ghosts?" "All of them." He gets in, his body warm for a change. No cold ass against me and him laughing.

PAST LIFE STEW. RECORD PAST LIFE MEMORIES ON TAPE AND MAIL AT RANDOM TO STRANGERS.

Sunrise brings dreams. Ken is riding a bicycle. He's holding a cigarette in his right hand, which means he's just had sex with the man at my kitchen table. I put my little plastic animals in a Pyrex baking dish and cover them with water. Suddenly the mammals will drown. How to pour off the water without them falling. I place a slotted spatula over one corner, but the animals slip through the slots. There's a big hole in the sink and the faucet is on full blast, washing them down. Frantic grabs. Steve calls wanting to talk about his magazine.

Kong

for Mike Belt

I meet The-One-Who-Won't-Fuck-Me for a drink at his favorite neighborhood bar. The walls are embossed with pink and gold waves: a room that never lets you crash to the pavement. Behind us a plaster nude holds a white neon ripple in one hand, her other feeds water to a half-robed hermaphrodite. The expressed purpose of this meeting is for me to get loaded and tell him my secrets. A round of rye and ginger, The One's favorite high school drink. At first it's strong and sweet, then only sweet. The One just had his shoulder-length perm cropped short and butch. I like it better, a minority opinion. I'm the heroine of his latest story: visiting the Empire State Building I run into King Kong. "Does this piece have *anything* to do with *me?*" I haven't been to New York since high school, let alone met a giant gorilla. Perplexity crosses his all-boy face, "I'm using your real name!"

Turquoise quilt with the stuffing coming out, I sit up in bed reading while my husband stares at the wall, the noir-ish venetian blind shadows. I nudge him, "Listen to this, it's sexy: *The male gorilla reaches out with both hands, swivels the female around and pulls her into his lap. He thrusts rapidly about two times per second. After about seventy thrusts he begins the copulatory sound — the rapid ooo noted in the previous copulation.*" As usual the husband only half listens — our marriage, like our Salvation Army quilt, has the stuffing coming out. Between us, a shrinking of time and an expansion of space, a hairy gulf full of breath and passion.

My friend Mike went to New York leaving me his key. I've just finished snooping around his bedroom — I felt like Goldilocks, trying out his bed — it was soft, though the chenille spread was brown instead of baby pink or blue. I forage some apple juice from the fridge, settle down on the nubby plaid sofa, and switch on the Sony Trinitron. Quel synchronicity! It's the 1976 remake of *King Kong*. I look at the giant husband, I mean ape, beating his chest and whipping his head from side to side as if his brain were on fire—then I look around the living room— then back at the drumming natives with bones through their noses—then back at the living room—and I am amazed at how Skull Island is Mike's idea of interior decorating: beside the white ginger jar lamp squats a black hairy thing hung with shells, feathers and rattle—its glaring red pupils stare right at me, tongue drooping from jagged choppers. On the bookcase, right above *The Best of Dear Abby* and the root-bound philodendron I'm supposed to be watering perches an Indonesian winged lion: bulging eyes tomato mouth razor incisors. Jessica Lange, covered with shells and twined to the sacrificial altar wriggles beside Mike's potted palm.

Miss Wray's clothes were pulled off by wires carefully lit so as not to appear in the shot. Then a waist-high model of trees, plants and rocks was placed in front of a back projection screen and one of the articulated models of King Kong was animated painstakingly so that its movements finally corresponded with the clothes, as they were torn off.

At the end of the bar a glass palm tree lamp, green and gold, shimmers like a jewel. The One recaps his research on the Baby Jesus' genitals in Medieval paintings. Do babies really get erections? Apparently the penis hardens but doesn't get any longer—"same with transsexuals," he says. There was this one notorious couple who had sex with this man who was straight with the wife and gay with the husband. After they paid for his sex change, he was straight with the husband and lesbian with the wife until the confused husband shot him. The man on the next stool picks up his brandy snifter, tries not to stare.

The male gorilla's eyes are closed, and the thrusts rock the female back and forth. His lips are pursed as the sounds grow more rapid, become slurred; her lips are also pursed and her mouth slightly parted.

Mike: blue jeans and a rainbow assortment of leather ties. We meet at work, share our anxieties like housewives do their babies. Our favorite is instant vaporization. Once I left a Nuclear War Survival Kit on his drafting table, a shoebox containing children's sunglasses (avert your eyes), a newspaper (cover your head), a can of generic creamed corn, and a band-aid. Spreading his fingers and shaking his hands, Mike squealed: we could market this!

I never realized how delicious rye and ginger is. If I drink enough of it I might get a grip on what happened between The One and me the other night, or, better yet, repeat it. He puts his finger in the V of my sweater and murmurs, "It's so low." I say, in mock exasperation, "I have a blouse underneath, so it doesn't matter." "Yes it does." *The tip-tip-tip of the iceberg* car engines on Market Street filter through the white lace curtains, Jessica Lange braces herself against Kong's hairy fist, shouts into his nose, "You damned chauvinist pig ape, you ought to eat me!" *This* must be the scene that drove her to acting lessons. *Even the very accomplished screamer Fay Wray could do little to upstage a monster fifty feet high, with a face seven feet from hairline to chin.*

The expressed purpose of this meeting: I get loaded and spill my secrets. *At about 120 thrusts the male gorilla suddenly opens his mouth with a loud sighing, "ah," and the female opens her mouth at the same time.* Dry-humping the mattress, my husband goes, "oo-oo-oo-oo-oo-oo-oo-oo-oo-oo-oo-oo-oo-oo-oo-ahhhhhhh!" The hippie Princeton scientist tells Jessica Lange, "He was their terror, the mystery in their lives, their magic." I heckle the Trinitron.

Quoting Oppenheim's fur-lined teacup Mike did a series of textured cups. My favorite is the X-Acto blade version, those triangular razors poking out in even rows like a deadly porcupine. Mike somehow manages to pick up the matching spoon. I cringe as he squints and snarls, the voice of a wicked old witch, "Come on honey, have some ice cream." As the spoon heads toward his mouth, he dissolves into wide-eyed innocence, high-pitched tremors, "Please, Mommy, no, I don't want any ice cream!" The wicked old witch: "Eat your ice cream!" "No, no!" Tears in my eyes, I choke out, "Sick, you're really sick."

"A nun gets crucified on an anthill?" "Honestly!" "Come on—a porn novel with the plot stolen from T.S. Eliot?" A new glass arrives. It is larger at the top and sits on a little pedestal. "Would I lie to you—it's from *The Cocktail Party*." "Speaking of cocktails, I really love this rye and ginger." Finally I pull out the secrets I've been stockpiling (my wanting to fuck him is the main secret, of course I leave that one out). He reciprocates by having sex with the bartender, right on top of the bar! The bartender's about forty, dark mustached, balding and knows we're talking about him. "See that thing he squirts soda out of?" It has a yellow band and says, "Schweppes." "Well, that had a big part in it."

Powell and Market, I look up from my history of horror movies and out the bus window: two old women are lying on their backs in the street. The 6 Parnassus didn't hit them, they were blown over! A strange swirling across the top of Twin Peaks—something *very big* is breathing there...limbs in midair, crumpled skirts exposing more than I am entitled to see, their hands grabbing for their purses, each mouth a stunned *O*.

That's not a hole you've just fallen into, it's a footprint.

Models of Kong averaged sixteen inches in height and were built of rubber and sponge over articulated metal frames. A separate giant mechanical hand was devised so that Miss Wray could be shown in his grasp as he pulled her from her skyscraper apartment. Postcard of huge-bosomed woman facing the Empire State Building, cartoon bubble from lips, "WHO'S AFRAID OF NEW YORK CITY?" On the back Mike's tall handwriting reminds me of my grandmother's, "Too much, too much, too much! It's almost painful."

The bartender yells, "Last call." Okay, one more for the road. When The One walks me home, will we do it again like we did last time? My stomach flutters just thinking about it: I leaned against the side of my building, then he leaned against me and we made out under the streetlight like a couple of teenagers. My husband was out driving his cab, he could come home or cruise by at any minute—but I didn't care if I was trashy—the smell of alcohol and cigarettes and that pointed tongue probing my cavernous mouth were all that mattered in the whole wide world. A woman in a bathrobe came flying down the front steps like a bat, yelling and shaking her arms in the air: I was leaning against the doorbell and with each kiss the buzzer would blast, rattling her out of her dreams *upstaged by a giant mechnical erotic ape* WE WERE CAUGHT a finger was pointing down from the sky and sounding an alarm.

Aboard ship Kong is imprisoned in this deep hole. As soon as Jessica Lange kisses the hippie primate expert her scarf goes flying across the deck, falls down the deep hole, and lands on Kong's napping nose. Sniffing her aroused hormones, he goes crazy. Poor Kong, his sad eyes, his six-foot smile. Ever since *Frances* I too have desired Jessica Lange. Baring her breasts with his thumb.

Mike returns from New York and takes me to breakfast at the Clarion, eggs scrambled with ham and bell pepper, sour cream on the side with a fresh fruit garnish. He unwraps two earrings from Trash and Vaudeville. "Here—I paid for the vampire bat but in your honor I stole the skull." Then he hands me a painting he did in high school: thick oil on a small canvas, orange and yellow mushroom cloud against a pale blue sky. To be hung above his drafting table. "Marvelous," I exclaim. "So orange! I always think of H-bombs as black and white because of TV." The oak table begins to shake, dishes rattle, linoleum rumbles. Heads drooped over cappuccinos shoot up. Crashing down Valencia, Kong turns the corner on 17th and lumbers towards Thrift Town, toes smashing cars and drunks, fur-lined heels cracking the urine-soaked pavement. Six point two on the Richter scale: ants, we are nothing but ants or worse, a nun crucified at the mound. Mike climbs out from under the table and squeals, "We could market this!"

The One jumps on the bar and grabs the soda nozzle, his twenty-three-foot arms having a reach of seventy-five feet. Helpful customers rush gold-sprayed palm trees behind him. He thrusts his articulated metal frame rapidly about two times per second, cocktail glasses rock back and forth. After about seventy thrusts he begins the copulatory sounds, "Too much too much too much…is happening…here…" His lips are pursed and the sounds grow more rapid, slurred. *I have topped The One – this has nothing to do with him – and I haven't used his real name.* A foot below him the arc of a gray biplane. The tallest building in the world, Sex has shoved him to the top without an elevator, who wouldn't roar and bang his hairy chest, one monster shaking another to its foundation. I miss the scene at the World Trade Center but I imagine: Kong thrusts across the roof, swatting fighter jets like mosquitoes. He slips on a CIA banana peel and crashes to the pavement below, not without one last longing look: close-up to Jessica's face, watery eyes, Kong is multiplying in her veins. She slowly turns away with the hippie ape specialist, "THE END" across their receding backs.

Hallucinations

The Passionate Robot

The robot rolls across the screen…a box of tubes and gleaming metal with a small camera-like head…definitely an "it". However, when Farrah Fawcett enters, this "it" changes into a "he" who begins to destroy the space station in pursuit of her *as if person could be shifted like a gear…or Farrah's hairdo*. Her blonde locks are futuristically straight: no more wings puffing back from her face in the *Charlie's Angels* style high school girls across the country copied for years. She looks ravishing in her white tunic, even more ravishing without it: never suspecting that desire could lurk beneath a chromium finish, Farrah undresses in front of the robot *her flesh so matte and crushable* suddenly a sound subliminal to her but creepy to the audience: the creaking of wheels: she turns around *mechanized fingers unclamp*. When the scientist disassembles "it," "he" puts himself back together and blasts through the laboratory doors, his telephoto eyes searching for Love in every pressurized corner. The scientist desperately tries to reason with "it," asking the question that's been on my mind from the beginning, "What would you do with her if you had her — did you ever think of that?"

About Face

The bully yells, "Take off your mask!" but the teenager isn't wearing one, the bones in his face thickening in the shape of a lion. Fortunately Cher is his mother, so he has a good mental attitude. Yes, she's low class and flawed *sex drugs cigarettes tight pants* but she can see the beautiful person beneath her son's bumpy surface — she named him Rocky like a difficult road or the popular ice cream flavor *he's so sweet and bumpy*. His girlfriend Laura Dern tells him he looks fine to her, but she's blind. They meet at handicap camp. The camera focuses on her serene probing fingers and I exclaim to KK *dear god please don't have him teach her what colors look like, the way they do in every blind person movie* as if blind people were obsessed with colors…likewise those paralyzed on screen are always wanting to dance…this makes them seem so superficial to me *blue is an ice cube, red a hot potato.* The blind girl squeals, "Rocky I understand!" In this country you never know where you stand—the ugliest thing at any time can make an about-face and become chic, like the '50s furniture strewn about my apartment.

Yoko

Bloomington, Indiana, the early seventies—I lie on my waterbed and smoke a joint with friends, mostly pizza delivery boys and waitresses. Then I crank up the Allman Brothers. Even though I hate the Allman Brothers. The grad student who lives upstairs raps on my door with tears in his eyes, "Please turn down that music. I have to finish my dissertation!" When I bought an album by Yoko he moved out. Her screeches rip though the speakers—it sounds like my stereo's fucked up, like some poltergeist replaced the diamond-tipped needle on the turntable with a safety pin. Yoko shrills like a wounded animal, like Janis Joplin's epileptic stepsister, her throat a ragged hole, a wrenching spasm ejecting emotion. Yoko wasn't the first rock star to insert the pretensions of Art into the popular arena, but whereas groups like The Moody Blues and Pink Floyd borrowed from symphonic music, creating a *Masterpiece Theatre* of rock that was overburdened with meaning, Yoko's pornographic rawness blasted through meaning. She was a wild-haired postverbal Cassandra, shrieking our impending fragmentation. I can't remember the name of the album, but I have a vague recollection of lots of green on the cover.

Full-Size Voice

KK insists on watching tonight's special hour of *Family Ties:* "Alex's best friend dies—it will be fabulous, a sitcom version of Elisabeth Kübler-Ross!" Skeptically I make myself a cup of chamomile tea and curl up on our rattan sofa with an afghan…sometimes cozy and domestic are all I want in the world, a privacy that's private just because it's too dull to tell anybody about. Before us a ten-inch Michael J. Fox with a full-size voice rants against the Inevitable, his tight little fist pounds a table and then the air: "I don't want to die I don't want to…I don't" *our deepest fears, as they should be, overacted, stylized…a cartoon.* A few months later this episode sweeps the Emmys.

He Could Live Next Door

The cathedral is massive…in its tower hangs a giant deafening bell…the hunchback swings from the cord sweating and snarling, a human clapper in the thunderous jaws of hell. More grotesque than his twisted body is his hopeless love for Gina Lollobrigida. With every major attraction, I have felt his despair myself, a mountain on my back full of warts and ravines no lover could ever have the strength to climb, my passion molten metal poured on the heads of the squirming peasants who jeer at me. *The Hunchback of Notre Dame* was the scariest movie I ever saw, even worse than *I Was a Teenage Frankenstein.* Nature's, not science's, creation, he could live next door to me — or closer — in my closet. Monsters hung from the hangers, festered in the convolutions of my sundresses — even with the door shut the hunchback crept out of there every night and my mother would have to leave my father and crawl into the trembling twin bed with me.

Beep Beep

In movies no matter how trivial a person is, when they die they are suddenly deep. And no matter how rotten they were to the other characters, we learn that secretly they were full of love. In *Light of Day* Gena Rowlands and her daughter Joan Jett are constantly yelling at each other and slamming things around, then Gena gets cancer and from her hospital bed she feebly vows, "Joan, you were always my favorite." Determined not to buy into her mother's trip, Joan cusses and acts tough in leather and torn shirts, takes a job as a heavy metal lead singer. To relax from her visits with her dying mother Joan haunts a video arcade, where she formulates the Meaning of Life: "beep...beep...beep." To Joan, each beep is separate. Buying into her mother's trip means believing they're connected. Gena, on the other hand, never lets go—in the end her altruism sticks to all of those around her like glue—tears well onscreen and off as she plans a comfortable future for her children and husband, undaunted by her failing brain and the conversations she unknowingly repeats as if her mouth's been pressed on rewind. Even Joan is moved.

Crowds

KK held me until I stopped crying, which is better than sex—certainly more rare. *I couldn't keep the movie inside the TV* an angry crowd chased me through the streets of Victorian England I limped until they trapped me in a train station urinal *a damp aurora borealis filmed the concrete* KK held me tighter as I spat out, "I am not an animal! I am a human being!" So I wanted to thank him with his favorite dinner: Nathan's all-beef franks on Wonder Bread and chocolate ice cream. The checkout line was long but I was fine—until I noticed the people, the weird people who shop at Cala Foods their faces blurred and angular the kind who don't have a firm grasp of the social contract I bumped into a woman's cart I didn't do it on purpose but she wanted to kill me *I felt as if the whole world were David Lynch's casting couch* I waited there surrounded by these people who, regardless of sexual preference or ethnic background, gave that group a bad name when it dawned on me ALL OF THEM WERE EXHALING DANGEROUS MOLECULES THAT WERE SEEPING INTO MY FOOD! The sun eclipsed above the frozen peas. I hurried through the automatic sliding doors, my thoughtful dinner fixings melting and spoiling in the steel mesh cart...I felt like a fool abandoning them...all that unrealized potential someone else would have to clean up.

Oral

The aging cosmetic mogul regains her youth through daily injections of royal jelly. But there's a side effect—each night she turns into the wasp woman and devours screaming wriggling people *beauty makes her crave the wrong thing* I feel sorry for her—she's such a wonderful human being during the day, spreading good cheer in a little black dress—all her employees adore her (before she eats them). The Blob is a monster as one-dimensional as an amoeba—it even looks like one. Nobody loves it. Slimy as an afterbirth shapeless as a force of nature it spreads across the screen like hips a seething excess of being sucking up good characters as well as the bad and the duds, famous Hollywood stars as well as extras, it incorporates everything in its slithering path like the worst postmodernist hack *technique without taste or discrimination* total yuck. In her suburban kitchen Meredith Baxter Birney stealthily stuffs party leftovers into her mouth with both hands. According to the TV Movie of the Week, bulimia is one of many social issues we all should be concerned about but which can be eradicated through group therapy. We recognize ourselves in Meredith, the eternal girl next door, Michael J. Fox's mother and before that Kristy McNichol's big sister—but the Blob is inconceivable a ravenous gooey pre-oedipal mass who if left unchecked will swallow the whole world—the addiction has burst free of the constraints of the addict. To my right KK feasts on a tub of popcorn and a jumbo box of Goobers, his hand and mouth smeared with butter, salt, chocolate—instead of glomming on to him during the gory parts I, in my very pale very stainable shirt, curl away to the left like a disjointed comma longing for its clause.

Audrey Hepburn

My world is dark, relentless as earth six feet under…but just because I'm blind doesn't mean I'm not an ingénue. My scream is refined, precise; my long famous neck so thin it fits into the crook of the murderer's cane. My wits are sharper than his dagger—I break free and smash all the lightbulbs douse him with gasoline maliciously strike match after match *a virtuoso display of touch and balance.* As I inch toward the front door, he throws open the refrigerator—the one bulb I forgot, its pale glow drowning my advantage…

Concrete

Imprisoned behind sumptuous brocade curtains Heidi wonders where her youth has gone; she yearns for her simple Alpine hutch, a paradise where she frolicked with peasants and goats. An evil Frau stole her in the middle of the night and sold her to this wealthy couple—as a pet for their daughter, the crippled Fräulein. Heidi wraps soft biscuits in a napkin and saves them for her frail grandmother. They will grow hard and stale, but it doesn't matter: Heidi's too pure to understand chemical processes *moisture, air, decay* the biscuits are her love: concrete: waiting in the closet white and flaky, manna for all our toothless gums. KK's arm drapes lazily around my waist, an umbilical cord connecting our two tired bodies, he tells me *Shirley Temple was sexually abused as a child.* Heidi's love raises the Fräulein from her wheelchair—golden ringlets jingling she takes the crippled girl's arm and urges, "You can do it," her lips puckering with each "oo" as if kissing a ghost…the Fräulein takes a couple faltering steps then runs in the sunlight for the joy of it.

Cowboy

A letter came in the mail from the Doris Day Animal League. Think of Doris in the original Levi's, tight, a red plaid shirt and kerchief at her neck, hands on hips, huffing in some sort of repressed sexual rage at a cute cowboy who will win her heart. Horses and chickens everywhere whinny and cluck with joy because Doris loves them. In the letter it said that it takes forty seconds to a minute for the stun gun to register, but cows are slaughtered at the rate of one every fifteen seconds, so that the terrified animals are gutted and skinned while still alive. Doris wants me to mail $50 to stop this.

Brain Tapes

I am unable to name the last four vice presidents of the United States—I'd rather watch a horror movie any day than read a newspaper—monsters are easier to take: pure sensation, affect that doesn't affect you, like the brain tapes Christopher Walken plays. Through his specially designed headphones Walken relives, viscerally and emotionally, other people's peak moments. The experience is ultra-holographic, stretching beyond three dimensionality to the...nonspeakable. Sex and family reunions are incredible, and you eat anything you want without gaining weight! Imagine, for ten minutes, not just to watch but to *be* Audrey Hepburn charming Paris in a Givenchy gown or the great Melina Mercouri as Phaedra slapping her maid *"I luff him!"* or the man with no bones melting to a puddle on the floor or the sea monster with a mop head chasing low-budget boaters *Gary Cooper waves to me at the station, "Goodbye thin girl."* Hooked up to the panel, Walken turns off the motor and respiratory controls in order to survive his colleague's heart attack. It's amazing the way a tiny button can make the difference between a vicarious thrill and annihilation. As expected, there's some suspicious monkeying around with that switch.

Double Dilemma

Before I learned to write, words were magic, imbued with the power to evoke Truth. How I long for those days of searching for the right combination of morphemes, fully believing that if I found it last night's lovemaking would reappear sinuous on the page, Life and Art connected at the hips like Siamese twins—the two of them have to stand behind a pole to look like separate people. Then it's easy to tell them apart: the brunette sister is evil and the blonde is good, or at least lucky: a man falls in love with her. The dark twin kills him in a jealous rage—the blonde has no choice but to watch, her sister's adrenaline leaking over to her side *a thick effervescence of anxiety and thrill*. What can the criminal justice system do? Send the innocent sister to jail? Let the guilty one run free? The part is played by real Siamese twins—a starring role after the smash success of *Freaks*—their wide-skirted gingham dresses are even more confusing than their moral dilemma.

Savage Grace

KK leaves a library book on my pillow *Savage Grace,* "HIS PARENTS ENTERTAINED ROYALTY. HE COMMITTED THE UNSPEAKABLE CRIME." I spy the word "matricide" on the dust jacket and crawl in bed with it for the day. On the cover photo the son in three-piece corporate wool sits on the sofa smoking a cigarette, on his right a leopard-skin pillow, to his left in pearls and designer suit his mother leans into the frame, sunlight from a penthouse garden, between them on the floor a shaggy white dog—their bowed heads point toward the animal's head, the camera's shutter has caught them with their eyes closed *somnolent halos shift and bleed, their souls have flown out the window to ShangriLa* page 342: son smashes mom's typewriter *trained to use the Latin name of the species he bred moths in her closet, dull wingy things that beat against her sables and Chanels* page 353: son dumps ice bucket down mom's dress *he rose from a tub of blue dye his skin a mottled aqua, then he went to the beach and covered himself with seaweed, said he was Neptune— in art class when he painted his nose instead of the canvas mom had to come and take him away* 366: son burns mom's furniture in fireplace *she was very Jean Rhys, flamboyant in old furs and feathers, green rings dripping from her fingers, her husband the plastics mogul called her an "atomic fly swatter," her son said she made him feel small as a lima bean, her favorite word was "marvelous," she wove devils' claws together to make a basket* 376: son tries to stick a pen in mom's eye *"the more complex the synapse in the brain," he wrote, "the further the curve to infinity"— in Mallorca the same thoughts entered mother and son's skulls, swelled and bounced off the walls, so big the house shook and they considered it unsafe to remain* 383: son pulls mom by hair, tries to push her in front of onrushing cars, breaks her finger in three places *son was a homosexual, when he ignored the women mom tried to fix him up with, she used her own body for the cure—sipping Dom Perignon she said "Oedipus" with the same sophisticated ease as "St.*

Moritz," but son found the sex sticky, he couldn't shake it off 369: son throws egg in mom's face and brandishes a kitchen knife — yolk dripping down her cheek she sticks out her chest and yells, "I dare you." On page 405 he obeys *he said it all started at age 3 or 5 when he fell off his pogo stick, he said it didn't matter because he and mom were one* the police found her corpse on the kitchen floor, the bloody knife on the cutting board, the police found son in the bedroom ordering Kung Pao chicken to go, "You know those little packets of soy sauce, can you throw in a couple extra?"

Stuck Up

I'm sitting in front of the TV with my lover (we're both in sixth grade, so This is a big secret) we're eating cookies that look pregnant *chocolate-covered marshmallow globs with a jammy red core* when the commercial cuts to an operating room. The doctors keep referring to the patient as ugly — hideously ugly — a woman too deformed to be seen in public — ugh! — though all we actually see are white sleeves, hands, scalpel, bandages. Twenty minutes later when the camera and doctors unveil the woman, I'm afraid to look, expecting a face that resembles a plate of spaghetti and meatballs — but my eyes register a beautiful blonde! In fact, it's the same actress who later becomes famous as Elly Mae Clampett on *The Beverly Hillbillies.* It's the doctors and nurses who are repulsive, their noses pushed up like pig noses. Afterwards, my girlfriend and I push our noses up like that and say scary things to one another, and we really are scared.

Creature

...they want to put his delicate skeleton in a glass case but he doesn't know he's exotic flickering with the seaweed oxygen tank beneath his horned spine hidden watching the beautiful scientist's legs kick and arc so long and pearly not even a callus on the heel his love for her is a green jewel its red ghosts shifting in the third dimension he has never seen anything so naked doesn't know his scales would shred

those thighs those wavering arms the blood fanning out in veils he
reaches up half flipper half opposable thumb opens at her ankle…

Hallucination

I found a remaindered coffee-table book of Diane Arbus'
magazine work, wonderfully grotesque portraits of Mae West,
Jacqueline Susann, tattoo artists, nudists, overweight
teenagers, and self-proclaimed lunatics. As Diane herself says,
"It's like walking into an hallucination without being quite
sure whose it is." I just *had* to have it. While I stood in the
checkout line a black man in full drag came up to me: black
Marilyn Monroe dress, black feather boa, tart makeup. He said
softly and luxuriously, "Do you know the nearest store where
I might buy some Wesson Oil?" I looked down at the book in
my arms then back up at him, felt unreal, as if the book were
talking to me, as if I weren't on Polk Street, but in a movie, a
monumental collaboration between Arbus and Fellini in which
they had secretly cast me as the leading lady, the wide-eyed
ingénue who bungles her way through a kaleidoscope of
abnormalities. The black Marilyn didn't fool me—I knew he
knew where to buy the oil—but I was impressed with him
nevertheless. Bad drag is always more stimulating than good
drag—it forces you to look through the illusion to the tender
details: smeared lipstick, one breast higher than the other, a
powerful jaw, heavy-handed eye shadow, runs in nylons.

Linda Blair

The bus ride is bumpy though relatively quiet…twin gleams of
turquoise satin come into focus, across from me sit a pair of
Asian grade school girls disguised as unicorns, frenzies of
lavender taffeta sprout from their compact equestrian bodies
mane and tail from each hooded head pokes a single woven
metallic horn. I'm afraid—but of nothing in particular—so I
stare at these girls cute as salt and pepper shakers turquoise
spats sliding around their four little feet. I keep waiting for my
subconscious mind/artistic soul to come to some conclusion or

witty summation to nudge these juveniles from decor to anecdote to myth...their costumes remind me of sleepers or snowsuits...matching mittens...nothing about them will open...I pull the bell and exit at Octavia, a blast of chill air distracting my thoughts in the direction of a khaki green mailbox which has been uprooted and twisted around backwards—I can't look at it without thinking automobile accident or Linda Blair's head.

Imitation of Life

The black girl denies she is black. The white actress playing her looks like Natalie Wood with lots of pancake makeup. "Passing." I found myself saying to KK, "That's how my mother thought of me"—in terms of the daughter's hoity-toityness, her fury to abandon her roots—my mother's disdain for my coffee grinder and modem, for instance. With race, difference is written upon the skin—except in the case of Sarah Jane. That's the plot. With class it's more a sense of inner corruption, caged but always threatening. In either scenario, the abandoner is the one who ends up feeling abandoned. "Mother!" she cries in a college-educated accent. Thursday as I was eating lunch in the Art Institute cafeteria, a sparrow flew in and rammed itself against the plate glass window. Art students carrying jackets tried to capture it, but to no avail. The sparrow hurled itself, over and over, against the glorious view of Fisherman's Wharf until it died. I pushed away my focaccia with sautéed greens, sickened.

Now Voyager

I dial my travel agent, a harried woman chirps, "Now Voyager, hold on please." Instead of muzak Bette Davis speaks, serious, dignified, mentally ill—she tells Claude Rains she'd be glad to assist with another patient, a sad little girl whose parents don't care about her—the agent breaks in, "How may I help you?" Just when I was getting into it. A week later when I walk over to the Castro a man stands outside Now Voyager asking for money, he's thin, thin as the crutches he's leaning against, upside-down Ls of aluminum with plastic cuffs to rest his forearms in, he pushes out a few words with the slow mushy inflection of a stroke victim, the only word I can make out is "quarter" — I shake out my coin purse and cheerily shove my palm at him, "How 'bout two!" Slowly he lifts an arm and takes the money, now he's monotoning something new. "What?" He stretches his arms out toward me and I hear the word "hug." He's wearing a backwards baseball cap and a peace sign, chances are he's gay instead of a sex pervert, and besides that I remember reading some article that admonished me to touch people with socially stigmatizing illnesses, people with cancer, AIDS, plus the other night I saw a movie on cable TV about Woodstock Nation. So I say, "A hug? Okay." Expecting a cursory little brush I lean toward him, suddenly he's doing this bear hug thing, his thin body pressed against mine his arms wrapped tightly around my back pulling me to him, I can feel his tibia pelvis sternum cheekbone...KK interrupts, "Did he pick your pocket?" "My pocket?" "He knew where your money was, and pickpockets are always making physical contact, like bumping you." "Yeah, but by hugging? I don't think he'd make much." KK gives me his take-a-look-in-the-mirror shrug. I shrug back at his cruel interpretation — but its appeal grows, transforming the man from heart-wrench to entrepreneur. *The untold want by life and land ne'er granted,/ Now voyager sail thou forth to seek and find.*

Bent

Taped to the ticket booth at Theater Rhinoceros is a warning THIS PERFORMANCE CONTAINS CIGARETTE SMOKE AND GUN FIRE German death camp the stage is minimal, painted gray, for an hour and a half our hero is starved beaten worked to collapse desiccated in summer frostbitten in winter forced to kick one lover to death forced to watch as another is shot forced to throw the corpse in a pit he jumps in after it his chest a bloody pink triangle he throws himself into an electric fence bent limbs akimbo like a Keith Haring icon FRY the lights dim — he's Bob Flanagan's brother Tim — afterwards we walk over to the Picaro to grab a bite but Tim doesn't feel much like eating, he hunches over the battered wood table nibbling a crust of French bread, he shakes his shaved head, "Thank god I'm in therapy while I'm doing this." KK takes pity, shoves a plate towards him, "Here—have some butter." He stares at the anemic yellow pad glistening with beads of melted ice *needs that only (an)Other's flesh can feed so pale…*

First Power

I found my lost earrings under the bed, put them on and went to the thrift store where on the New Arrivals rack I found an Ann Taylor silk blouse that was so stunning I no longer wanted the flannel shirt I was wearing—why not switch them like infants at birth—after all used is used what's a little sweat under the armpits. Inside the dressing room I took off my tired rag and was about to put on the dazzling soon-to-be purloined blouse when the hanger caught my earring, knocking it to the floor an earring with a conscience silver and amber with slivers of African trade bead…earrings I'd given up on but they returned, were reborn imported from the East like an exotic religion. The First Power is the power of resurrection… Homicide can't get rid of the plump-lipped serial killer, when they execute him he bounces back to life possessing street people a cop in the department. An exorcist nun tries to stab herself with a mystical implement half crucifix half dagger but the plump-lipped serial killer flings it to the ground the First Power is too strong he hops out of the nun's dying bosom and chases a red-haired psychic who in real life is Melanie Griffith's sister.

Revenge of the Nerds

"They say nerds make good husbands." Overweight, nearsighted, scrawny, black, Asian, gay, stubby or giant, nerds spent their childhood summers at computer camp; they're proficient on the accordion. The nerd community, in its rejection of aesthetics and social hierarchies, is far more radical than a fashionable arty underground. Nerds glory in consumerism, yet remain tasteless as communists. Using their towering nerd IQs they unlock the secrets behind electrical gadgets and program them to do their bidding—a closed-circuit TV network is secretly installed in the snobbiest sorority, nerds gather in their dorm lounge to watch—they zap the monitor with their remote and bedroom after bedroom appears with coeds getting undressed *bare tits and string bikinis* nerds gawk and drool as a squat robot rolls among them dispensing brightly colored cocktails. Nerds are kind of magical—like witches. On the dance floor gyrating their awkward out-of-shape bodies, belching, nerds offer a vision of freedom unimaginable to the uptight fabulous others who watch on, appalled. Nerds are the last reverberation of the hippies, the freaks, though in spirit only—in the '60s nerds still would have looked like nerds *gawky glasses and greasy hair* you'd never see a nerd wearing wirerims. Nerds fuck whenever they can find it, they fuck like me—with abandon and gratitude. And afterwards they're loving and loyal. "Once you go nerd," confides the former prom queen, "you never go back.

Knowledge

An ambulance woke me abruptly with its wailing. I felt a dull pain in my groin—my pubic bone was bruised but I don't remember bumping against anyone or anything in the night. Do you think visitors from outer space with red and yellow whirring lights stole me away and did sexual experiments on me? Years later a pale little creature with a gigantic head will appear in my dreams, will rasp out, "Earth Mommy." In the sequel to *Rosemary's Baby*, though the Satanic cult members make him drink Evil from an ornate chalice, Rosemary's son is too pure for the devil to possess, the followers can't even coax him off the sacrificial table until they play some rock music. Then he floats around at a party glass-eyed as a marionette, like Peter Fonda on good acid in a '60s "art" film. I switched it off before the end, but I bet you anything the devil didn't win—the best he ever does is to get set up for another sequel. Anyone is a potential victim—the most ordinary people are probed by huge-eyed aliens. "The better to see you with," said the Big Bad Wolf. I don't believe the inside, the physical, has any secrets to be unlocked—either you are possessed by it reduced to a few gasps and feeble attempts to claw the air or you try to turn the tables, contain it with metaphors and measurements: hot flutters ninety-eight point pressure rushes two centimeters dull shooting shortness one hundred and postnasal urgency palpitations quickly stars.

FX

As I brush my teeth I watch an actor being blown away, he hurls himself backwards on a couch wrenching and writhing with each imagined impact, I'm impressed with the precision of his timing, the gymnastic flips of his chest and hips—but the BANGs are out of sync with the FX so that the bullet shots echo rather than precede the "bloody" crater-shaped explosions in the actor's dress shirt—the blasts seem to be coming from the man himself as if he were the shooting machine, the bullets ripping out of his chest and into the camera. I try to point this out to KK, but with my mouth full of toothpaste the words emerge garbled and mushy.

Slaughter High

The school dork, blown up in Chem Lab as a practical joke, now haunts the high school reunion. His face looks like Play-Doh gone insane. How typical. What's odd about this film is that it's made in England, but masquerades as an American movie. The British actors impersonate Americans by guzzling beer and throwing their bodies around like deranged Texans. KK and I giggle our way through two hours of bloodbath: linguistic hybrids are hung by the neck, impaled, dunked in a claw-footed tub of acid (skin foaming and sputtering like Mr. Bubble), crushed, slashed, poked in the eye with a hypodermic needle. My favorite is the gum-chewing blonde in bubble hair and fur stole who plays the wife of a wealthy '80s businessman with the finesse of a '50s moll. No explanation is given for the double bed on the second floor of a high school—the moll/housewife sneaks up there to fuck her old steady *anemic flesh and her large drooping breasts bobbing up and down* she grabs the metal headboard which ZAP electrocutes her (the school dork must have gotten an A in Shop) the blonde's deathbed histrionics remind me of Judy Holliday having a nervous breakdown. No matter how much the director slathers on the gore, it can't compete with the actors' outrageous accents: New England, Virginia, the Valley and British idioms jumbled together in a single sentence, the effect increasingly uncanny, like some dialectic DNA has begun to unravel.

Riotous

When I was in high school the Chicago Convention Riots were the coolest thing to invade my suburban TV, passionate young people shouting and kicking, with cool hairdos and even cooler outfits, hauled away in paddy wagons STEAL THIS BOOK! Years later when I moved into the city I acquired a boyfriend who'd been arrested in the riots—only he hadn't been protesting, he'd just been walking by and the "pigs" grabbed him. The boyfriend didn't believe in politics because it interfered with other people's karma. The Jews killed in the Holocaust, for instance, were working off karma in a big way. They would come back in their next lives as better, freer people. I guess the invasion of Normandy fucked that up. My boyfriend's ex-wife claimed to be a walk-in from Venus. She used to go on radio talk shows and discuss the advanced educational system on Venus. This is a true story. When I moved to San Francisco, I got caught in the White Night Riots. I was walking home from a friend's house and suddenly I was confronted by a line of smiling cops in riot gear. Oops! I wished I were a cartoon character, like my legs would turn to wheels, and I would zoom away WHOOSH! leaving a dust trail behind me. When I finally did make it back to my apartment I rushed to the TV and turned on the news: long shots of cars in flames, close-ups of teary faces and battered skulls, I searched through the masses of extras in the background, but there was no sign of me.

Delinquent

It's not easy to love a delinquent girl.
She's vulgar, she's coarse. She despises the world.
—*G.B. Jones Retrospective*

Throughout most of the movie she is a victim of
monstrous schoolmates and a monstrous mother, but
when, at the end, she turns the tables, she herself
becomes a kind of monstrous hero—hero insofar as
she has risen against and defeated the forces of
monstrosity, monster insofar as she has herself
become excessive, demonic.
—Carol Clover on *Carrie*

Paint was covering everything. That must mean that I
destroy either myself or the world whenever I fuck.
—Kathy Acker, *My Mother: Demonology*

Dear Kathy,

At Nayland's dinner you explained the dynamics to me: the
bottom (you) is given permission by the top (whomever) to be
bad. "Run down the street naked." "Okay." You can't be bad
on your own because you were raised to behave, to curtsy to
your mom's rich friends. I imagine a tiny homunculus of Kathy
rotating on a pedestal as she recites Miss Manners' rules of
etiquette like Bible verses. Here's a sick story from *my*
childhood: when I was four and a barking dog frightened me,
I climbed into my father's arms and cried, "Daddy, why don't
you shoot that son of a bitch!" As my mother recalls this, tears
of laughter come to her eyes. Beyond occasionally washing my
mouth out with soap she didn't try to civilize me. I grew up
with no internalized wall of Good to bounce my Bad against—
maybe that's why I've never seriously gotten into S/M. "Run
down the street naked." "Fuck no." All those instruments,
those contraptions of containment—I'm more of a natural type
of gal, morality flopping around me like a fish out of water.

In white gloves and ruffly slip little Kathy worshiped the girls who were bad:

> *Bad* means *slimy* or *dripping with sexual juices* thus *messy* and *mean*. I knew that the rankest possible sperm was drooping out of the lips of these girls. While mouth sperm flowed in them, their hands moved under their skirts. They weren't awake without masturbating. They masturbated everywhere except when they were getting screwed.
>
> I knew that the girls were dirtier than all these images.

I too was dirtier than these images. I used to crouch in the alley with the boys, rolling and mashing damp sand into lumpy cylinders we threw at one another, "Here, have a turd!" Giggle. "Fuck those mud pies!" Giggle. We talked dirty to establish dominance. My father was a construction worker—I could spout obscenities those boys had never heard. "Wow, Dodie you are so cool." Thus began I to use words to show off, to woo.

> Later I would meet girls who actually were as wild as I thought boys were. Girls carrying cunts who breathed, like those monstrous clams I found on ocean wastes, slime each time they opened, the way I know a heart will if it's separated from the body: the vulnerability of openness.
>
> I hadn't yet met a boy, except for a cousin who couldn't play basketball as well as I could, nor had I met one of these girls: I didn't need actual beings to know that they existed. And I knew something else. That I was akin to them because I was wild, but that my wildness consisted in my lack.

The wildness of lack: not an assertion of self but an emptying of self. Your badness rages around a void, the place of no-Kathy, the cunt. Things tumble into it. *The knife which was the extension of the murderer pierced her flesh. The flesh around the entry line became a cunt.* Like a command the knife penetrates the girl and the girl swallows back. *Your enormous lips are greedily parted and you secrete saliva like Pavlov's dog. Crying out for all of it, yes, and then wanting more, you wail.* In place of the self is an ever-renewable insatiable hunger, a chasm that devours the world: an obsessive buffet of indistinguishable lovers, the contents of a room, somebody else's story, a psyche, the master's blade. Writing is an eating disorder—you/it gulp(s) down the Brontës, Argento, Dickens, Leduc, Faulkner, Laure, von Sternberg, de Sade and spit(s) them back up. What comes out comes *from* the self but is *not* the self. *Beauty will be CONVULSIVE or will not be at all.*

Gulp.

Feminism failed because women are thieves. Never having owned anything, not even their selves, they filch texts…souls…dreams…space. The text has no power over its own violation, thus its name is WOMAN.

When I was in junior high, bad girls rode the bus downtown to drink cherry cokes and to steal. They sat at the back smoking Kools and popping bubbles round as their teased heads. One girl purses her chalky pink lips, pulls out a tasteless wad of Bazooka, grinds her cigarette out in it and hurls it at me. In home ec Miss McMorrow says rats and roaches nest in her hair, in her never-washed AquaNet hair. Wrapped in candy-yellow angora her boyfriend's ring bulges from her finger; her stomach is flat as the Gene Pitney and Dion 45s stuffed down her stretch pants. When a bad girl flirted with another's boy, a skirmish would erupt in front of the school. Tits flopping back and forth like punching bags SLAP SLAP the girls kicked bit and scratched 'til they drew blood, pulled out crackly tufts of ratted hair. Eager for a glimpse of girdle or bra strap the boys rallied yelling, "Catfight! Catfight!" Afterward they patched their nylons with thick globs of nail polish that blotched their calves and thighs like a contagious disease. The hems of their wide cotton skirts were turned under half a foot or more and roughly stitched in place. Bad girls didn't trim away the excess material because they were lazy. I was lazy myself but bad girls didn't interest me, they were too much like my mother, coarse and old. Whenever I raised my hand in class they hissed, "Shut up!" I was more like Carrie, the mousy weirdo who looks up "telekinesis" in the card catalog. An intellectual. Eventually the girls got pregnant—their cunts were made of bubble gum, sperm blew inside them swelling their bellies enormous. The boyfriends took back their rings.

In writing it's so easy for the worm to turn. Take the evil carnival crackpot...ZAP...he's a chicken man squawking in his own shit.

I'm sorry I used your affair with the Zen monk in my Mina letter. It's just that you exude a daring and panache that wallflowers like me only dream of. You and the monk, me and Kevin—we couldn't get into the Kafka movie because *Premiere* had given out twice as many passes as seats. Weaving through a mob of drips who kept bumping into one another desperate for their freebies I said, "Damn!" Whereas you, your shaved head swiveling across the overflowing auditorium, smiled and announced, "This is a very Kafka experience." See what I mean? Did the monk really have a picture of a Thai girl with a Coke bottle up her cunt? *All that is left is sex alone and its naked violence.*

Re: appropriation: my pastiches are the misdemeanors of a bicycle thief, while you Kathy Acker are grand auto all the way.

> I realized that I no longer understood any customs or laws.
> The realms of Death, where I've never been, have customs and laws which I don't know.

Who tells you to be bad in writing? Who commanded you to write "Clit City"? *Its walls were painted with manure. I was the only human here.* Did Heathcliff, or better yet, Dario Argento appear to you in the night, "Write this down, slut!" *The taxi driver pulls cunt hairs out of the surrounding flesh—part of the cunt's mind thought, I want to get out of here—"The school," she said, "was burning down." No. Our cunts.—she saw gigantic cat's*

*eyes looking at her and touched the bottom of the cross, her cunt —
blood streamed out of every part of her and made all of the apartment
smell like bleeding cunt — maggots were coming out of my cunt
because maggots come from meat — houses are cunts — maggots don't
come out of cunts because maggots can be born only in dead flesh — I
will come into the Sacred Heart of Blessed Jesus which is truly a
cunt — cunts just want to be cunts — that's a cunt not a girl — in my
dreams the cunt was triangular: Father, Son, and Holy Ghost — in the
swampy regions of the cunt Charon rowed and plied his boat as if the
skiff was a finger reaching up — Circe's cunt can summon up night,
chaos and death.*

The text is Daddy and everything else is Mommy and you are
the incredible voracious hole. Appropriation is another name
for incest. Gulp.

> I tried to end everything: to lose myself, to get rid of
> memory, to resemble whom I don't resemble, to
> end… Sometimes when I encountered myself, I was
> so strange that "I" had to be criminal — all the time I
> was totally polite and, simultaneously, my language
> was brutal, filthy,
>   I meet a star
>   go and am there.

It's chic these days to toss around "transgression" as if it were
an English word in a foreign language. Kinkiness as a cerebral
exercise pisses me off — poseurs flaunting their tit clamps their
"difference" — let's mutilate them let's destroy them let's suck
their blood and spit it on the ground. As the Haitians told
Maya Deren, "When the anthropologist arrives, the gods
depart." Behind the transgression of obscenity, pleasure
protrudes, "My cunt is a camera," the simple sensuous
pleasure of rolling those words across my tongue and lips.
You're right, Kathy, we could all use somebody to tell us to be
bad. Mina Harker speaks through me, the voice of the vampire
goddess — I sit down at the computer and pretend I'm in the
alley with the boys again, "There's this really neat trick I do
with sand."

You run away from childhood like you flush a huge turd down the toilet – the taxi driver is a snob, the shit in my asshole – the dog shit right here becomes you – the headline said "BAN ABORTION" into the shit that was gurgling out of the black and brown gratings – when she came to she found herself lying in a shit pool that wasn't going anywhere – two young girls are tranquilly shitting into the holy water basins – she spurts bits of shit forth so that the altar breaks into pieces beneath her – we'll shit on you because you as politicians taught us what shit is – you fucking shitting skunk of a bumblebee – at last it is clear that the Church reels in its own shit and that every text is a text of desire.

Shit is the oxygen of your literary atmosphere. The cunt is the mouth that breathes it in. Sex is a nightmare of effects: narrative discontinuity, abrupt changes in position and lighting, unexplained losses, confused durations – a writing with the primitivism of a stag film, that "seems to want to remind viewers of their position in the theater or at the smoker, on the edges of a frame that cannot be fully 'penetrated,' witnessing a spectacle that still has aspects of what could be called a (genital) *show* rather than identifying with actions of a temporally sequenced (genital) *event*." (Linda Williams, *Hard Core: Power, Pleasure, and the "Frenzy of the Visible"*) Our expectations fester, bleed, dissolve. You're so good at being bad in your books that some fools assume you're a dominatrix – straight men who need to be set even straighter. "I'm not a top, hon," you drone matter-of-factly, "That's not what I'm *into*." As the Haitians told Maya Deren, "He who wears the shoe knows best where it pinches."

Life doesn't exist inside language: too bad for me.

My dynamic is more like this: I'm bopping along minding my own business and some people go *insane*. I could never understand why Miss McMorrow hated me. I eagerly cooked and sewed for her, and I always wanted to wear dresses, the frillier the better. I looked like a small tank in them but I loved them. Once I played Slaughter in a white blouse and wool sheath. The boys and I divided ourselves into two gangs, lined up facing one another, and when somebody yelled "Charge!"

we raced and tackled. The side with someone left standing was the winner. My mother found me in the backyard writhing against some boy with my skirt hiked midthigh, kicking and biting like the mutant offspring of Audrey Hepburn and Godzilla. She freaked, "Dodie, you can't do that!" She grabbed my elbow and started pulling me back to the house. "But Mom, my team was *winning*." From behind her humongous glasses Miss McMorrow squints her squinty eyes, her frizzy red hair squints too, she shakes her finger and hisses, "Tomboy!"

I don't belong in the normal world whose name is sanity.

I threw down my flat-chested Betsy McCall and exclaimed to my best friend Pam, "Lets pretend we're boys today!" Skipping down the alley we hooted cusswords, climbed fences and dumpsters, knocked stuff over, pulled mildewed *Playboys* out of the garbage. I taught her how to make sand turds. When Pam went home filthy and disheveled, and confessed all to her mother, she wasn't allowed to play with me anymore. *"Listen," I whispered to one of the female variety, "if you think that your vaginal smell is better than a rosebush's, you're kidding yourself."* Kathy will at least go to the movies with me. Sometimes. You leave a message on my phone machine, "Sorry I didn't make it to *Army of Darkness,* but we just started fucking and I got majorly distracted." BAD. "It was fantastic."

Let your cunt come outside your body and crawl, like a snail, along the flesh. Slither down your legs until there are trails of blood over the skin. Blood has an unmistakable smell. The cunt will travel, a sailor, to foreign lands. Will rub itself, like a dog, smell and be fucked.

When Toronto artist and rock singer G.B. Jones visited my apartment one Thanksgiving she left behind an extra-large Fifth Column T-shirt and a fine orangy smudge of face powder on the phone receiver. Makeup is powerful. She lifted a pale hand and in her husky baritone whispered, "Call me Gloria." When I met the other band members I was surprised at what nice well-scrubbed girls they were, bouncy and jokey, writing quirky messages on anything I would push in front of their faces—it was like having an autograph session with the

Monkees, like having the Monkees in my very own living room—a far cry from Gloria's rendition on the T-shirt, tough girls in studded leather pouting up tons of attitude around a motorcycle, their poses aggressive and rough as G.B.'s technique, a drawing with the oomph of a prison tattoo. *I can only be concerned with the imaginary when I discuss reality or women.... Bad means slimy or dripping with sexual juices thus messy and mean.* G.B.'s glorification of the women-behind-bars mode echoes the philosophical confusion at the end of *Grease,* when Olivia Newton-John makes her glorious metamorphosis to black leather—if good becomes bad, could bad really be good? This bending of categories leads to what is for me the central question of postmodernism: what's the difference between a moral stance and fashion? Over my head I pull the stretchy white tube of the T-shirt. Gulp. I am swallowed by Art. I look down at the screened images—upside-down Caroline's face is as large as Gloria's torso. Directly beneath my chin a tiny skinhead guy floats behind the girls, his right leg growing out of the top of Caroline's head. I think of a line I stole from an artist on PBS: "Perspective gave us the artificial feeling we could get away from things." In G.B. Jones' drawings perspective is subverted—rather than allowing you to get away from "things," she fists them in your face. Good and bad battle across my chest until my breasts feel like two brothers on opposite sides of the Civil War. The coffee I spill on the T-shirt falls, appropriately, in the shape of an exclamation point beside Gloria's full spiky bangs. Wearing this T-shirt I dream killer mosquitoes have taken over the world, but there's an AIDS convention in town and it's discovered that AIDS blood will kill the mosquitoes and save humanity—this is a far cry from the popular monster antidote of '50s sci-fi: seawater, an ordinary substance, a simple liquid, innocuous. I sit up bare-assed on the edge of the bed scratching my forearm. Bad. Good.

I wish you had met her.

Love,
Dodie

The Flowers of Mina Harker

"Get rid of those tulips," she screams, "They're trying to kill me!" *The lady lies against the lipping water, supine and indolent, a pomegranate, a passion-flower, a silver-flamed lily, lapped, slapped, lulled by the ripples which stir under her faintly moving hands* jasmine flowers call out his name in the night, gasp "you're great" in mint julep accents *a valentine of dried roses and grass, it looks like a wreath you'd see on a pet's grave* my cheeks bloomed to a blush my mouth swelled crimson *to represent the cunt two women stand side by side pretending to be flowers unfurling as a red-clad woman moves back and forth between them* three-tiered cake crowned with wildflowers *I found a skinned rabbit in the basement sink its muscles gleaming rose-gray* its beauty scared the shit out of me *I've seen her purse her lips like red bouquets toss off sexual predilections with the ease of naming her favorite flowers* cockscomb, virgin's bower, night-blooming cereus, vanilla, winter cherry *a few months later Leslie and Cecilia will fill this same space with flowers stick a label on the phone* Beverly Hilton *tails bloom like tropical plants pupils widen blue vision sweeps to black* he rose from a tub of blue dye his skin a mottled aqua, then he went to the beach and covered himself with seaweed, said he was Neptune *swallowed in a frenzy of percale flowers and wild strawberries Dodie cups her breasts and mumbles* the cemetery is full of cats, plastic flowers, and pictures of the dead leaning in gilt frames against crumbling and ornate Christs *roses daisies mums, stems hacked off* purple red pink red purple red *orangy sap of blue and yellow whatnots splatters across a choppy green field* purple red *who decapitated all these flowers* red mercerized flowers reflect the blood-drenched Argento poster *he kissed me on the cheek and I felt frumpy in my droopy orchid corsage* he sucks my flowery titties nylon mesh scratching his tongue *a man has to learn to take the rough with the smooth* facing a packed auditorium, with a large orange flower arching from the back of his chair and over his head, he listens attentively to Charles Bernstein's vigorous delivery *take it/ every atom of me/ belongs to you/ across distances/ one space* penciled eyebrows and ruby lipstick cheapen my repose though the tiny garlic blossoms about my throat are innocent enough *the ugliest lamp sits on the nightstand coarse red swirls on frosted glass, red roses* red rhymes with dead *KK lays his head on my breasts and rubs my ass he's so* dexterous *behind him a bush is loaded with flowers mottled green and white like poorly tinted Easter eggs* so I gave him a bouquet of flowers (the transitory) and a fossil (the eternal) hoping that like night and day there would come that rare cosmic instant when there wasn't any difference *she sits before a hand-painted antique mirror, pink and blue flowers frame a blonde organism that others seem to recognize* worm on the rose *bullets bloom in Raymond Chandler's chests* a pregnant woman sits across from me in a smock with a Peter Pan collar, a field of wildflowers shirrs across the yoke and billows about her global belly *unspoken, the possibility shimmered between us like the Dickens novel I'm always raving about but never get around to reading — or the horizon on one of the travel postcards Sam sends me, the Arizona/Hawaiian/Thailand sunset blooms orange and pink as if the world were a flower, fingerprints faintly dot the skyline like UFOs emerging from the fourth dimension* wish you were here *the flowers her husband placed beside her bed are stunning, large waxy trumpets, white with deep red throats, she thinks of broken hymens as she pulls the covers over her shoulders and instantly falls asleep* my palm stings as his ass blooms bruises and his cock hardens *my legs are covered with bites which bloom into wildflowers* gardens blooming from her armpits *you lean closer to examine the last decadent flowering of Dion's flat stomach* so what if we both were married, my desire was clean and sharp, cutting through all the practicality crap — he was a radiant compassionate animal hung with ribbons and flowers *alas, and round this center the rose of onlooking blooms and unblossoms* Quincey folds his hands under his head the pale hair of his armpits gnarling like cauliflower *who needs brains with that ash blonde widow's peak rosebud navel that beigy-pink mouth with its mysterious smirk* given a nurturing environment, I could have made the transition to a nice unencumbered fuck *daisies come to mind rather than heavy-headed roses or the operatic odoriferous freesia.*

Sex/Body/Writing

"a fairy tale assumption in which an all but non-existent condition is assumed to be rampant"
—Samuel R. Delany

The accused is permitted to display the bumper sticker EAT SHIT because it is determined that no motorist, not even a coprophiliac, is likely to be sexually aroused by a bumper sticker reading EAT SHIT.

arousal = criminal

nonarousal = noncriminal

Offensiveness is outside the equation. When I write, "My cunt is a camera," is this likely to arouse photographers, the scenic vistas of my camera's wandering eye—or the filmstock itself?

I'm working toward a writing that subverts sexual bragging, a writing that champions the vulnerable, the fractured, the disenfranchised, the sexually fucked-up. A female body who has sex writing about sex—no way can I stand in front of an audience reading this stuff and maintain the abstraction the "author" A BODY some writers glory in this but I feel miserable and invaded—as if the audience has x-ray vision and can see down to the frayed elastic on my panties. But, really, it is I who have invaded my own privacy. To regain some of that privacy I have desexualized myself in public, have stiffened, as if to say, "This is not a body."

To a five o'clock cocktail party in Berkeley I wear a black Italian pantsuit with a pink silk blouse—because that's the way the women dressed at the last five o'clock cocktail party I went to, at the French Consulate. But in Berkeley everybody's in linen, jeans, sandals. Joshua Clover is casual chic, lanky as a cornstalk, all in white—white linen shorts, white shirt, flame white hair, single silver hoop in his ear. Standing beside him, I feel like a black bat. "I'm having some problems with transgressive writing," he says. "Why is A.M. Homes so popular? Because she's transgressive without being challenging." Transgressive but not challenging YES these words circle through my head like a mantra for days—a formula for just about everything that pisses me off. Any sentence containing the word "gender" is at the top of my list.

EAT SHIT NO/BODY

F., I have heard, rejected a piece of mine because it contained too many body fluids. Two years later, I run into him at the Small Press Traffic mailbox. He shows me a favorite passage from Blanchot: the poet must expose himself to the violence of pure being. Or some such thing. "Yes," I say, "but how do you then go to work?" F. explains how he thinks one could juggle that. He's sweet today, so shy, so halting, so "I'll lick your boots." A guy confusing as Lon Chaney—the clownface dissolves to disgruntled scientist dissolves to clown—HE Who Gets Slapped (MGM, 1924) gets the last laugh. I don't know what to think of him. I smile, say, "Good luck on your thesis," and walk down the stairs.

A physical body writes about sex.

H. sits at the back of my prose workshop, sullen alienation brooding in the corner. I take one look at him and think, "Oh shit." His attractiveness is not wrought from art school pretension—it's more of an afterthought—if that. H.'s writing deals with schizophrenia/paranoia/madness/psychological disintegration. "i live with monsters who are contagious," he writes. "the transmitter planted deep inside my ear instructs the following: i, to justify misfortune and misery of fallen angels, is chosen to sacrifice you to unknown forces that make cars move." I ask him personal questions he refuses to answer, but I keep asking anyway. I learn he's Korean and his family's in Los Angeles. That's all.

In one piece a woman gets too close to him so he eats her. It's his "Archiving" assignment. "Choose an object that you can easily bring to class. Write a real or imagined narrative explaining this object's significance — its importance in 'your' life, how it came to be a part of 'your' life. Type and make copies for the class. Bring your object with you." He brings in a plastic fork and knife.

"the smell of her boiling flesh invaded my room. she's here no longer but she's here with me. the plastic fork inscribes embryo, the plastic knife paints pictures of her memory. what can i say, i've fallen in love with her."

I don't let on *how* drawn I am to this writing, but H. seems to know anyway. Over the semester his manner softens to sweetness, eagerness, affection even. The one day he's not in class I miss him. Unanswered questions, I suppose, are a form of intimacy. He writes, "you, standing middle of my target, i can admire you more than physics allows me." I know this isn't about me, but I pretend.

I do a little makeover: lose some weight, streak my hair, spend teaching money on new clothes. T., whom I haven't seen in months, walks up to me at a party and says, "You look really good." In the past he hasn't given me the time of day — even though I've made overtures. I think, "I hate you," get out of the conversation as quick as I can.

The last day of class. S. has changed her hair from white blonde to yellow blonde. "I was looking too '80s." S. projects a desperation for attention that she doesn't have a clue how to get. (My soft spot for her.) Finally, after hinting about it all semester, she's writing directly about being raped. "in the back of my head lingo had long since departed and I wasn't prepared to go down" This form is really working for you, I tell her, the straightforward narrative interspersed with poetic intensities. I think to myself, "This woman, this BODY has been raped for Christ's sake." While Creative Writing teaches us thus to hermetically seal content in aesthetics, I'm thinking, "Dodie, you are so full of shit."

The time is up and I say, "Well, we're finished — in a big way."

H. blurts out, "Want to go out for a drink or something? I need some closure."

Writing that shifts the matrix, e.g. Samuel Delany's *Hogg*. "What it seriously attempts to do," Delany explains in a 1989 letter to Randy Byers, "is challenge just about every dichotomy on which our culture is based. And the distinction between dirty and clean — as a grounding for both civilization and pleasure — is one of society's most fundamental." And then, "*Hogg* constantly compels the reader to choose one filth-laden situation *over* another, when most of us would simply want to be rid of the entire set of experiences."

Fountain pen scribbling across paper, a body writes about sex. Sitting at the computer, a body writes about sex. The keyboard and monitor are enormously erotic THE BEEPING MODEM, THE WORD MACHINE TALKING BACK more than once email has gotten me in trouble.

I wake up to a shock of wet at my feet — Stanley, my cat, has peed in the bed while I was sleeping in it. "I'll deal with this later." I get up, make coffee, sit down at the computer and take some Delany notes — "hebephilia, the love of filth" — I'm reading and typing and thinking about Delany for an hour or so when the scent of cat urine impinges upon me — the gray jersey nightgown I'm wearing reeks with Stanley's urine. How marvelous, I think, Delany has imbedded my woof and warp NO DISTANCE WOOF AND WARP I toss the nightgown in the hamper, throw on another thrift store favorite, this one with "Neiman Marcus" in huge red script down the length of it, and continue typing.

Tell Somebody Something
You've Always Wanted to Tell Them

September 17, 1999

Dear Michael,

Last night I dreamt that something was pounding on the door of my hotel room, pounding so hard the door and the wall *dusty maroon* slanted inward, an inclined plane, I stepped into the hallway, and behind another door I saw a makeshift morgue *blood and oozing splatters* a half-dozen naked men slouching in claw-footed bathtubs. In David's painting *The Death of Marat* the dead hand clenches the death letter signed by Charlotte Corday *am I Charlotte Corday? I don't think so* I woke with a start and stumbled into the living room, the slatted closet door was cracked open, glowing from within, or so it seemed *my flesh* I crept forward and saw the illusion, light reflected from the edge of a window shade — things were normal but the threat still lingered *maroon image* I turn on the overhead in the kitchen, peek in the bathroom, my office, the toilet on the back porch, I rush back to the bedroom, check that Kevin's still breathing *he is* but the threat doesn't leave me.

When I begin to type "Dear Michael," Word 98 flashes a suggestion in a bright yellow box, "Dear Mom and Dad," a subliminal prompt to hit the return and Word 98 will do the writing for me *my father is dead.* When John downstairs became a junkie he started letting *them* into the building, through the window of his back porch *no shades* I used to watch this guy, sores dotting his face, shoot up *blood stained white hanky, four spoons placed in the shape of a cross* one time he was striking match after match and holding the flame against the cluttered wooden floor, it was winter and the porch was unheated but he wasn't wearing a shirt, as he bent over his jeans drooped far down, I stood above him leaning over the balcony, peering at the long curve of his pale ass, he stopped moving, stood there contorted from the waist, deathly still. The match burned down to his fingers, he held the pose for minutes, held it longer than

I could stand the cold, I darted inside. This is how I think of you, Michael—out there with me on my balcony, watching *meat on the other side of the plate glass.*

Last Sunday afternoon, half a block from my house, a guy approached, sneaky he was, waited until he was right upon me before he started yelling—vicious—I couldn't take it all in but I did pick up "you bitches" and "pussy" I glanced at him and pivoted to my right as if directed by remote control, eased in a diagonal across 11th Street, pretended I hadn't noticed *civilization is a border littered with needles, condoms, broken car glass stench of urine flaring your nostrils* since moving to Minna Street I've seen dozens of cocks hanging out of pants, some spewing liquid, others not—one night a guy swiveled round and displayed His to both me and Kevin *upping the ante* I stared straight ahead my eyes wide and vacant as the Children of the Damned, but Kevin studied It, his gaze languorous, lascivious. The guy didn't do anything and we continued to the pizza parlor. I've seen people fucking shitting giving head smoking crack *the basic human body position is hunched* but only four women, in eight years, pissing *turquoise bikini sagging from ankles.*

"So what's your favorite term these days," asks Bruce, "for doing the deed?" We're on the phone and I have to pee. "'Shagging?' 'Bonking?' 'Schtupping?'" "I don't know, *Bruce*— 'having sex'? I never talk about it, I'm not *writing.*" Why did you ever call him? I think. "So you just stick with your old favorites, 'screwing and fucking'?" When you went to see the Bill Viola show in New York, you told Kevin, Viola's slowly dropping water beads so excited you and Judy *the tension* you rushed back to your hotel and fucked. So, last weekend when I finally saw Viola's droplets swelling to the breaking point then slamming onto the amplified drum I thought of you fucking Judy *swelling and breaking* I couldn't see your bodies, just this blurry back and forth *pinkish smears* it was three in the morning, the museum open all night for the show's closing, the floors of the darkened rooms were scattered with reclining twenty-somethings, lying on backs, sides, propped up on elbows, they looked like well-dressed aftermath, you had to step over them to see the art.

Tubes of flesh trail me beyond the periphery, do I really care about them? Not really.

You like *things* I can tell by your shiny black shoes, your miniature movie camera, but images satisfy you more—you film me on my back porch *three minutes without moving, like one of Warhol's screen tests* I use the time to scan your body slowly from foot to head, a compact body, tense, somewhat uncomfortable, black shoes, black jeans a bit too tight in the waist, that little ineluctable gap of zipper beneath the snap, I think of it often, that taut half an inch, straining, small belly where your black shirt tucks in—recent, I imagine *born in 1962.* Back in Vancouver you photograph my letter and my USF ID— for a prop you buy a shoulder bag you think I would carry, and you mock up a crime scene, scattering Imodium tablets, the latest Danielle Steel, a small notebook along the ledge of a ditch *yellow police tape DO NOT CROSS* afterward you wipe the mud from the ID's bar code *because you like things clean, you say* you send me your passport photo taped to a pornographic nine of hearts *featuring Superslut Nikko* ebony thigh-highs baby blue prom garter purple scrotum *both breasts and a dick, that's a surprise* the Filipino tranny looks genuinely happy *mouth agape* taking it up the ass from this all-American blond guy with a cock as big as a sea serpent's tongue *locked nest* you look washed out and kind of wasted, your greased hair poking up like spider legs *but still attractive, of course* Michael's passport to what? *no message without meat* you scrawl your name across a page with a bold red marker, the marker *says* presence, but I wonder. Bruce's theory of social schizophrenia: it's like a black hole: chaos builds, dense matter/dense psyche tumbles inward, an onrush of density IN too much density dense dense space bursts open a ray (of sperm, Bruce laughs) shoots out and shudders the earth. The time I spent in Milwaukee with Ed— things were going fine until I got my first period, then he recoiled from me *what's your problem* I said, but his problem became my problem *blood condensing on sheets, thighs.* You have me flickering in super 8, Michael *I imagine it in black and white, is it?* but I have you in words, you're mine *molecules lacy as lint* eventually a breeze will sweep across this page.

Love,
Dodie

Doing Bernadette

for Bernadette Mayer

October 1, 1999

Joel,

I'm sitting here sneezing like a son of a bitch (that's my father
speaking through me, the most vulgar man who ever lived, I
used to say if they deleted the word "shit" from the English
language my father'd be struck dumb, I hate the word "bitch,"
hate how suddenly I hear guys calling each other "bitch" in the
movies on the streets on the buses, I guess '70s feminism never
totally died in me, more like it was buried alive, screaming,
jocks spit this femaleness back and forth, actually it's kind of
funny, because no matter how macho they spit it, white guys
snapping "bitch" sound gay, like Kevin Spacey in *American
Beauty*, okay he doesn't say "bitch" but he might as well, when
I asked Kevin K. what he thought of Kevin S., who we all
know, at least in my crowd, is gay, Kevin S. playing the straight
guy to all these gay men, Kevin K. said he didn't believe it for
a minute, that Spacey's middle class disgruntled husbandhood
was pure bitchy/queeny, like Richard Burton in *Who's Afraid of
Virginia Woolf?*, how George and Martha were really a gay
couple, a simple transposition of gender, Edward Albee)
anyway I'm sneezing like a son of a bitch because the slacker
skateboarders downstairs chain-smoke and the fumes come up
through the floor, a whirring black box behind me blows
"clean" air, it's cold against my arm, thank god, because the
past few days it's been hotter than a son of a bitch, why am I
thinking of my father today, it's no special day, my mother in
this dreadful pink jacket leaning over his coffin crying and I
refused to go up to the front of the room and look at him, the
only dead people I've seen are my father and his father, the
Western dead are always on their backs, a rather female
position, don't you think, like we're all in the missionary
position to meet god, like we're all bitches before the great

father, the great unknown, they had this holy roller preacher there which incensed me because my father hated religion, and according to the preacher's schematics (not that he said it in his sermon, not with the crying widow beside him) my father was bound for brimstone, and for a moment I was in terror that he would snag my mother into being a god awful Christian *invasion of the body snatchers* and then I'd lose her too, but that didn't happen, as you know my mother's taken not to religion but to gambling away her pension, the preacher read that "the lord is my shepherd" thing, we in the folding chairs in the funeral home with its piped in muzak versions of hymns were the lord's sheep "he leadeth me beside the still waters" the preacher said this was an example of the lord's wisdom and beneficence because bubbly waters irritate the sheep's noses, so the lord leads them to still waters so they can drink without their noses being irritated and this deep laugh started in my stomach rose to my chest up to my throat I clenched my teeth my lips shut and turned bug-eyed to my sister-in-law, she looked back at me like isn't this disgusting but she didn't share the bug eyes, nobody did, and I felt so alone so alien in my humor in my black wool sheath and navy blue silk blouse, clothes too warm for a midwestern June but I didn't have anything else, and my mother in that glaring pink jacket, she's turned vulnerable since he died, tells me her fears wants to please me, the last time I was home (when I didn't see you) she said, "I don't want you to be bored" and I was shocked and a bit revolted, this coming from Ms. German-Taurus-Raised-During-the-Depression-with-an-Alcoholic-Father who as long as I can remember has waged a one-woman war against my feelings *life is rough you do what you have to STOP YOUR WHINING!* I wasn't bored, loved hanging out with her and her friend Stella, we went to "the boat" and my mother handed me $100, "Gamble your little heart out," she said and I won $240 on the poker machines and got to keep the original hundred so I can't complain and then we went for Mafioso pizza in Calumet City and laughed our asses off, Stella with her white hair and my mom with her pink lipstick, our waitress was befuddled and inefficient and when I mumbled some tacky crack about her Stella leaned across the booth and said, "You're precious," and I took that in and I held it and I thought they were precious too, the longer I was an arts administrator the more I understood my mother, the administrator isn't allowed feelings, the administrator smiles and holds it all together, all those fucking divas doing their histrionics around me, when I graduated from college the only job I could get was serving food in a dorm cafeteria, I'd stand there over the steam table in a horrid starched yellow uniform and hairnet, red faced, sweating like a son of a bitch and all these students on the other side of the mashed potatoes complaining about their fucking tests, my mother was a cafeteria lady in my high school and that's how she got the money to send me to college, at the time I didn't think irony, I thought karma, her toil and what a fucking brat I'd been, I can't stand poetry readings, can't stand poets, have this adolescent longing for real people, real life, whatever that means, which means I spend most of my time alone, some with Kevin (not really I see people all the time but I only think about myself and Kevin, nobody else sticks) when I got up this morning he was wearing a dark purple pin-striped shirt, I brushed his arm, rough cotton dense flesh, he threw his hands in the air and said "purple haze" then he left and I made coffee and toast and sat down at the computer and turned on the email that's when your group message came up, you've moved it said, is there a story behind that — the frailty of your relationships *how's Catherine* — or simply a better place? I noticed the zip code had changed and you seemed so enmeshed in Wicker Park, I imagine answering the email and the studied distance of your response, and I'm like why bother, and we used to be so tight, uncomfortably so at times like the waistband of my Gianni pants and then Lynne Tillman left a long black hair on your car seat and suddenly you were like *Dodie who?* I felt like an old shoe and snarled back "star fucker!" only psychically, of course, I'm too *adult* to shake up such drama *lips zipped shut* and it wasn't even *real* stars like Mark who's writing his memoirs, William Burroughs was timid and thin as a young boy, he was in his 70s and Mark in his teens and it felt like two boys in bed, I'm going over to his place this afternoon for a tarot reading, he drew two cards on my phone machine, the first card he said meant chaos but it's just temporary because the second card said that, cosmically, things are going really well for me.

Love,
Dodie

Reading Tour

New York, St. Mark's Poetry Project, April 29, 1998

The Bronx, Kevin and I are in St. Raymond's, the church where the Lindbergh baby's ransom money was dropped off. Kevin's showing me the different crannies, the baptismal, the organ loft, the altar, the reliquary, and then we get to the candles you can light for the dead, several rows of clear red tubes on tiers. The "candles" are inside. Kevin puts a dollar in the collection box and presses a button. Up comes a flame. I ask him who the candle is for. "All the people who died of AIDS." That evening at a wedding reception we dance alone to "My Funny Valentine." The lights of the hall are dimmed, and high above us the ceiling glows the same red as the candles, helium balloons snuggle against it, metallic hearts left over from another party. Kevin and I twirl clockwise until I grow dizzy. I'm resistant to taking this scene anywhere, to nudging it into meaning: Tragic Mortality. The red rhymes, this is what matters. And, I guess, the human connection.

In Chelsea we buy sandwiches and lunch on the docks with Joe Westmoreland. Decaying concrete and no shelter from the sun, a yacht shaped like a bullet slips by. Joe tells us how Charlie used amateurs in his porn video and the amateurs couldn't keep hard. A few feet away an aging man wearing headphones and a white string bikini throws his arms over his head and dances. After three years Joe's having his Hickman catheter removed, he's excited. His emails detail the effects of his medications, lead runs through his veins one week, then his energy increases and he gets lots of writing done, then his vision blurs and he has to stop. During the final chase scene in *The Peacemaker*, when the Bosnian tries to blow up Manhattan with the nuclear bomb he carries in a blue backpack, an aerial camera zooms over these docks. "Look!" exclaims Kevin. "That's where we were, with Joe."

Travel poetry is the worst, at more than one reading about Italy or South America I've whispered cattily s/he never should have left San Francisco.

Washington, D.C., Ruthless Grip, May 2, 1998

At the Vietnam Veterans Memorial we see ourselves reflected in the shiny black marble, ghosts among the wreaths. With a pencil and a sheet of notebook paper a woman makes a rubbing of a name. Kevin cries.

Mark Wallace says to me, "Dismemberment and disembodiment…they're the same thing!" It's been a long time since I've felt this understood. We're at Stetson's, which, they say, is Monica Lewinsky's favorite saloon.

Chicago, Columbia College, May 5, 1998

O'Hare, 2:30 in the afternoon, sitting at the regional bus terminal across from the Hilton. A woman walks out of the hotel in a black strapless evening gown with a floor-length skirt that poufs out from her hips. Around her naked arms is draped a black shawl, a string of jewels sparkles around her neck. She looks like a black princess. On the other side of a plate glass window in my immovable seat and wrinkled travel clothes, I watch her with the awe of a child. A limo arrives, and a man in a tuxedo takes her black gloved hand. My mother got to ride inside a stretch limo and she said it was fabulous, couch, TV, bar, phone, everything. She was across the street sitting with Anita on her front steps when a limo pulled up. The driver was a friend of Anita's husband, just stopping by. Anita winked at my mother and said, "How about giving us a ride around the block." "Sure." Anita's husband was appalled, but the two women laughed and climbed on in.

I'm resistant to ideas here, I just want to create analogues. Analogues can be very powerful, can make the body spurt juices.

My mother's house, a two bedroom green-shingled house with

a third bedroom added when it was deemed Joey and I were too old to share a room. It's raining hard so I step out on the front porch to experience the fullness of it, but protected. Across the street a couple of houses down I see a dark figure, a man near the curb, leaning against an elm. There's such a stillness about him, he looks like a silhouette cut out of the downpour. He has one leg bent at the knee, the sole of his foot pressed against the tree trunk. I think I see him move, dart back inside, peek from the door—a figure so wooden, so dark, so ominous *noir invades suburbia* a stranger who could lock children in trunks, an anybody who could rip out hearts while they're still beating. I call my mother, "Look." "Oh that thing!" She rolls her eyes. "I hate that thing, it smokes a pipe, it's so stupid." She says you buy them at lawn stores. I don't admit I thought it was a real person. Lawn figures are popular in Hammond, particularly lawn geese, three-foot high concrete geese which housewives dress up for holidays—lawn goose with Pilgrim outfit for Thanksgiving, pumpkin outfit for Halloween, Santa-suited lawn goose. The lawn goose on my mother's front porch is wearing a gray hooded sweatshirt. "For the winter?" I joke. She tells me of a neighbor's lawn frog that was stolen. A week later the owners received the first of many photos mailed to them anonymously, photos which ultimately documented their frog's cross-country vacation, the lawn frog at the Grand Canyon, the lawn frog in San Francisco with the Golden Gate Bridge in the background. Her favorite was the frog on a plane, framed by the faces of two smiling pilots. The pictures were published in the local paper. When the frog's vacation was over it reappeared in its yard. The next night my mom invites me to "go to the boat" with her, one of the casinos floating on Lake Michigan. Her favorite, with a Mardi Gras theme, is docked in East Chicago across the road from Inland Steel. She seems unmoved by the mill, a megalithic monster sprawling for blocks, spewing out smoke and pollution into the night sky, while I in the passenger seat grunt, "Wow." She points to a building, "See that smokestack that's spitting fire…that's where your brother works." Joey, who is a crane operator, sits in a compartment that hovers above molten vats. The compartment is refrigerated, so he's considered lucky. He got bladder cancer in his thirties, a disease usually limited to elderly men. He blames it on the poisonous fumes. As our four-door pulls up to the casino parking garage, above us, 400 feet in the air, looms a huge oval sign glittering with flashing lights. SHOWBOAT. Behind it, in the background, industrial hell. My mother still has my late father's handicapped sticker, so we get to park right by the door. (He died last summer, but it's good to the year 2000.) For these people, I think, there can never be too much gilt on the lily—clothing on a lawn goose, slot machines with skulls that double your winnings.

Tucson, P.O.G., May 9, 1998

During our final descent into the Tucson airport, Kevin points to a tumbleweed and starts singing, "I've got spurs that jingle-jangle-jingle." I can't stop laughing.

We get to spend the night in the Poet's Cottage, the University of Arizona's adorable adobe guest house for visiting poets. On the bookcase in the living room is a guestbook with poets' signatures dating back to 1992—some are dead, most I've never heard of. Susan Howe stayed for a month. Tom Centolella hailed from the Bay Area. Many poets have added ecstatic compliments about the cottage. In the living room is a couch, two easy chairs, a coffee table holding coffee-table books, a large gas heater poking out of the fireplace. The mantle is loaded with religious icons, Christian and Native American—Virgin Mary candles, little brightly painted human-shaped things. Two walls are lined with framed broadsides of dreadful poems, things like "when I grow older my words will come from a distant place deeper inside myself." Lots of useless linebreaks. References to saguaro. Being forced to live with these broadsides, I conclude, constitutes Poetic Ritual Abuse. No wonder there's so many empty wine bottles in the utility room. From the coffee table I pick up a small clay animal bank, not any animal you'd recognize from nature, but the bank reads as animal nevertheless. The bank rattles as I turn it upside down. No cork on the bottom, I guess you have to break it to get the coins. *How poetic* I think, unkindly.

The Poet's Cottage is better stocked than a bomb shelter—hammered metal mirrors and lamps, candleholders, sunscreen. The Holy Bible. Clock radio, TV at the foot of the bed (no cable), 4 clear channels, lots of ghosts. Southwestern tchotchkes galore. Screen door, front porch, patio in back. Shelves of poetry books in dining room and study, in the living room a case of books on Arizona history, nature, and culture. Three boxes of Kleenex. A barbecue grill, bag of charcoal, and a typewriter on the closet floor. Central air conditioning. Refrigerator containing peanut butter, bottled water, coffee (decaf and regular) and two jars of premium fruit preserves. It's as if the poetry fairy godmother has anticipated all the poet's needs—toaster oven, Mr. Coffee, coffee grinder, assorted black and herbal teas, spice rack, two boxes of crackers, honey, olive oil, assorted utensils including a vintage eggbeater, wire whisk, barbecue fork, corkscrew, pots and pans, plates and bowls, lots of coffee cups. Wine glasses. Herbal shampoo and conditioner, Curél Daily Moisture Therapy Lotion, three packages of dental floss, toothpaste, typing paper, drawerful of University of Arizona envelopes, lawn recliner, dining room table, double bed, dresser, tea kettle.

There was no dingo saliva on the bloody, tattered baby clothes, no dingo fur either. Cat hairs. Because of this the dingo baby's mother goes to jail. The traces are so minute. My mother saw a TV show that examined the dirt and debris in a "clean" hotel room. Under ultraviolet microscopic sensors, traces of shit were everywhere, on the phone receiver, the door knob. Sperm was sprayed on the wall. "Yuck!" she shook her head and stuck out her tongue. In the Poet's Cottage, Kevin and I are sure that sperm is sprayed on the walls. This gives us a good chuckle. There's something creepy, zoolike about the idea of a poet's cottage. In the morning we're awakened by animals hooting and howling. Coyotes? Mocking birds mocking coyotes? Mocking me?

Everywhere I turn in the Poet's Cottage, poetry closes in. I'm desperate for prose that isn't about Arizona. Finally on the coffee table I find the Afro-American poetry and prose anthology from Penn, turn to an excerpt from Jean Toomer's

Cane. I haven't looked at Toomer since the '70s—it's a description of a woman he's in love with, a lazy trashy woman whose name starts with A, but Toomer seems more interested in describing the landscape than her. I'm intrigued by this woman and the way Toomer's subjectivity obscures her. More of a perfume than a footprint. I feel so Laura Mulvey *male gaze* until I remember a poem I wrote in my 20s, a scathing poem about my Vietnam vet boyfriend. He tossed it back at me, "This poem isn't about me it's about you." He was brutal, but he was right. Around that same time, for a date with a poet I wanted to fuck I bought a flowing white blouse woven with thin metallic threads, the fabric was rather sheer and I was aware my naked breasts were visible beneath it. Sitting across from me in the Universal Cafe he said, "That's a perfect poet's blouse." Later that evening he took it off. Life was good. Now coyotes are mocking me.

The condiment bar at the Tucson McDonald's offers jalapeños and salsa. Walking over there I bump into a cactus, the kind with flat, paddle-shaped pads. Instantly my right forearm and elbow are loaded with short red prickles, thin as threads. Kevin pulls some out with his well-developed nails and I want to lick him like a grateful German shepherd. Since the hair on my arm is also red, I have to put on glasses and lightly brush my arm with a finger to locate the remaining prickles...prickle...a coarser, stinging analogue of my own hair...oh no, I'm feeling a poetic moment welling up...the metaphors start

> festering, the lines start
> breaking I
> want to write a poem a-
> bout riding on the back of Daddy's
> Harley whizzing past
> saguaro though I know
> not what a saguaro
> is.

On the way home at an airport gift shop I buy a refrigerator magnet, a howling coyote carved out of some lightweight stone, with TUCSON etched in its tail. A charcoal-colored crescent moon is attached to its body with white cord, three colorful plastic beads are strung on either side of the moon. A fetish(y) object. Kevin, who's of the opinion that refrigerator magnets should be tacky, says this one isn't tacky enough. I tell him he needs to broaden his definition of tackiness. The head looks more like a long-eared pig than a coyote, a howling long-eared pig, hole poked in the stone for an eyeball, it's on my refrigerator right now holding up a recipe for Tomato Butternut Soup.

San Francisco, Small Press Traffic, May 15, 1998

Subjectivity as an enfant terrible…ravenous a different kind of poetry reigns among San Francisco's avant-garde: deepness has been replaced by smarts. The experimental poet who proclaimed, "I just had an exciting intellectual exchange!" What happened to "conversation" I wondered. It's such a burden to have to pull off smart, it certainly silences me at cocktail parties. "Secret dinners are held in the East Bay when important poets come to visit." I stare vacantly out my bedroom window at the overcast sunset. Dark gray mass edged with pink, and then the gray dissipates and I watch a salmon-colored lamb float upward, turn into a dog. The frog beside it turns into a centaur. In the Poet's Cottage I'd wrestle out a symbol; in postmodern San Francisco I'd refer to Wittgenstein. Now the pink has all gone and I follow a faint gray bird skeleton, the higher it rises the whiter it grows, the bluer the sky. I think of the time we went out to dinner with Phoebe Gloeckner and her husband Arthur Suits, a research chemist at UC Berkeley. Kevin asked him, "Arthur, what makes the sky blue?" And I asked him, "Why isn't the sky blue all the way down?" Passing the Kung Pao Chicken, Arthur recalled the "old classroom exercise" where you place a drop of milk in a glass of water and the water looks blue, it's about reflection and density. Something, I can't remember what, isn't dense enough close to the ground, that's why it's not blue down here. I looked at Kevin and he looked at me, our looks said that neither of us had ever seen or heard of anybody dropping bits of milk into blue water.

Beneath me in the doorway of the Euro car shop a homeless man sits on a pale blue blanket, writing on a sheet of notebook paper. Above his head is painted NO PARKING ANY TIME. He's very intent on what he's doing, doesn't look up at me like most people sitting on the street do, like they can sense my stare. He's a regular—a tall, thin, attractive, black man who wears a gray cloth wrapped around his head in a low turban. He's propped a large section of corrugated cardboard on its side in an L-shape as a shield against the wind. His office. His legs are outstretched, with a *Bay Guardian* on his lap, the notebook paper on top of the newspaper. His desk. His dark blue pants have sharp creases but are too short revealing his ankles. His black running shoes are untied, never any socks. Once I saw him eating Cheerios out of a plastic bag. At night his cardboard office, flattened and laid on the sidewalk, becomes a bed. Sometimes, he places it on top of his outstretched body. A roof. He stops writing and studies a small publication that is printed in two columns. Then he begins writing again. I could get rid of him if I wanted to, all I have to do is dial 553-0123 and utter the words, "Homeless encampment." But I never call the cops, even when his shouting wakes me at night, I peek around the window shade, he's alone down there, pacing in circles, his mouth going a mile a minute.

"So what's this piece about," Kevin asks me. "Just that you feel out of it?" In *Mimic* an autistic boy embodies the romantic notion of the artist, the lone soul outside of society wrestling with beauty. The boy sits by the window, watches insect men stalking humans. As he rocks and clicks soup spoons together his face remains impassive. He calls them "Funny shoes." Not "insect men." Because he can name the brands of everybody's shoes. He points to famed entomologist Mira Sorvino's feet. "Nine West." "He's good at this," she exclaims. Details open to him, he makes delicate wire sculptures of the insect men, and when he's captured they don't eat him. He wanders among them, a terrified mascot, clicking those spoons. I can relate to him so, yes, I guess I do feel out of it. When Johanna Drucker read here she talked about the self-censorship she inherited from the San Francisco avant-garde, the squelching of her narrative impulses, and I could relate to that too. *Life is so enormous, thin-skinned, thick-skinned, sometimes, but not always, gleaming.* In bell hooks' *Wounds of Passion* the biggest crime is not being able to speak her mind. I was struck by hooks' unflinching belief that whatever's on her mind is of urgent importance. Speaking one's mind, that's what an essay is supposed to be about, right? My mind spoken. What happens to a mind that is spoken? Does it become a ghost? Do you lose a speck of mind when you speak it? Does it spout wings and flap off like the evil stepmother's raven in *Snow White?* Does an irrevocably changed trace remain? White letters on black T-shirt I pass on Castro Street:

> Respond
> Release
> Regret
> Repeat.

San Francisco, Book Party, June 7, 1998

After ten years of writing it and three hard years of finding a publisher, *The Letters of Mina Harker* is finally out. I'm standing in Norma and Rob's dining room in my wedding reception outfit, a severely simple black dress and a vintage choker, a wide garland of multicolored rhinestones that sparkle beneath the spotlights, I'm holding a bouquet of roses, my smile bursts from ear to ear like crimson popcorn, and everyone is applauding *slow motion hands float through the air like bubbles* for me, Dodie Bellamy—it's the ecstasy and wish fulfillment of Carrie at the prom, sans the pig blood. That was my fantasy. But in actuality, and at the same time, it's like being submerged in a giant fish tank, with fish after fish swimming past me, a whole highway of fish bumping shoulders and wriggling, their round lips mouthing "congratulations" or "great necklace," and I need to thank and engage every fish, to make each and every fish feel welcome, special, appreciated *Doug Sam Nicole Sonia Laura Nick Yedda David David David Rodrigo Bill Mara Barbara Leslie Hung Suzi Brian zoom zoom Garrett zoom zoom zoom Jeff Aaron Dale Steven Alvin Jack Cole Stephen* the room feels bright despite the overcast day *Colleen Jonathan Michael Nathen Pam Lauren Matthew Fran Spencer Nick Peter Eric Mac Lew Rob Rob zoom Wayne Elliot Cliff Scott Jocelyn Mary Glen Molly Travis Susan Steve Susan Myung Terry George* and on and *zoom zoom* and on. Of course I miss half of them. And the dumb ass things I write in the books they hand me.

Jacqueline Rose: "Once a piece of writing has been put into circulation, it ceases — except in the most material sense — to be the property of its author." Yes.

My dream of becoming the Queen of the Avant-Garde — was this some inflated vision of fate — or did I merely fall in with the wrong crowd? In 1982 when I entered Bob Glück's writing workshop I had reached the end of my '70s feminist rope, had fled from my women's workshop, where my writing was seen as the product of a sick mind. "Look at all this sex and violence! Have you considered *therapy?*" When I found the gay New Narrative perverts ("More sex! More violence!") I dove in headfirst. I was nondiscriminating, would attempt any fashionable technique — without question or even sympathy, wildly changing persons, tenses, collaging stuff, making lists in the middle of a narrative. I was insanely jealous of the praise Bob gave to a schizophrenic poet named Marsha. Marsha's syntactic leaps came to her as easily as breathing while I struggled so painfully for mine. My mind was this logocentric street grid *stop signs, right angles* while Marsha's was wavy gravy. Disjunction was cool, and my whole life I wanted to be cool. Like Sylvia Plath I've always been a conformist.

In biographies a writer comes in contact with a certain group or person and his or her work clicks into the *right* direction and destiny is fulfilled. In high school I worshiped Gertrude Stein, the surrealists, my fantasy of Joyce. Also Robert Kelly's *Controversy of Poets* anthology, which I devoured with almost zero comprehension. How such attractions grew in a working class girl in Indiana, an isolated and miserable girl, is a mystery to me. At sixteen I wrote in my diary, "Sex, religion, literature — these are all that matter," and clearly I was predisposed to become a trippy sex writer — but what if I'd fallen under the spell of others during my formative years? Would I now be down-home as Dorothy Allison, epiphanous as Jorie Graham? If I'd been a petty thief in L.A. would've I become as hard-boiled as James Ellroy? If I'd spent one more night in Tucson would I wake up the Poet of the Saguaro? "I know what you mean," says Kevin. "People go to Naropa and they become Naropa writers, people go to Bard and become Bard writers...who knows...what would have happened if we didn't end up in San Francisco...it's creepy to think about." He's sitting on the edge of the bed, I'm slouched against the wall, over my head hangs our "Barbara Steele diptych." Kevin grabs the side of his head and silently screams in mock horror at the randominity of it all.

While I believe — really believe — that formal innovation opens new vistas of expression, better allows me to track a psyche's collisions with a fucked-up misogynistic culture, I'm still plagued with self-doubt. Am I an elitist, I ask myself, am I like one of those social climbing neighbors my mother scorned, the ones who traipsed around with shopping bags from Marshall Field's when Sears and J.C. Penney have everything a reasonable person would need? Is my mother right about me, have I become too big for my britches? Or is it merely a matter of context? I'm thinking of the young poet visiting from New York, who when asked, "Would you like some Chardonnay or Sauvignon Blanc," quipped defensively, "I don't know anything about wine." A response that surprised and charmed me. It's just part of the culture here, I reassured her — wine is everywhere, they grow the grapes here, bottle it. Sauvignon Blanc versus Chardonnay — it's like asking if you'd like a Diet Coke or a Diet Pepsi. "There's a big difference," she said, "between Diet Coke and Diet Pepsi."

In Dutch

I stare out my office window as dusk begins to fall over the campus, the soft shadowless light brightening colors. Languorous curving pathways cut through the crayon green lawn. A small fountain spurts cheerily above a bed of neon tulips. Plump little birds chirp with an opulence I've never heard in the city. I need to begin working on my poem for the Vermeer section Bob's editing for *Plough River Review*, but I feel stuck, uninspired. On the phone last night Bob seemed surprised I'd never written a Vermeer poem. "Everyone else— Brenda, Jorie, Claudia, Joshua, Lucy—already has one—or a whole manuscript of them—lying around. Doug Powell has written a Vermeer suite." Another reason they're all so fabulous and I'm . . . just here, adjuncting, my last volume *Fat Ghost* rejected by Wesleyan. I need to be more timeless. I stare at *The Milkmaid* jpeg I downloaded and begin to type.

> After Vermeer's Milkmaid
> by Carla Moran
>
> Hair hidden beneath her linen headdress, breasts bound,
> the sturdy young woman holds the pitcher in both
> hands, her head tilted downward
> prayerlike, her focus singular, milkward. Light
> floods in through the many-paned window, mysterious
> and precise, glazing the room with presence.
> Last night I dreamt I was pregnant, my insides
> luminescent with new life. Six months—too late
> for an abortion, so I held my tumescent belly with both
> hands, warmed to my fate, to the task of loving
> this young star throbbing within my womb.
> The milkmaid pours her milk with such determination.
> It is her duty. Her mind, her soul flows in its whiteness,
> warm, fresh, musty-sweet as baby's breath.

I didn't plan for the pregnancy thing, and the abortion suggestion—is that too controversial? I'm sure Bob would be fine with it, but I've heard rumbles that the dean thinks my writing's too edgy. A knock startles me and I swivel around in my wooden chair. "Come in." There in the doorway stands the student in all his glory — long sideburns, button eyes — I've seen a string of young women fluttering before him. He receives them with the casualness of someone who's never negotiated, only chosen and received. "Am I interrupting anything?" "No, no," I say as I quickly save and close the poem file on my computer screen. "I just thought I'd stop by and chat. Got some time?" "Sure, have a seat." He sits down on the bench behind my desk, and I scoot my chair to face him. "What do you want to talk about?" I say. He shrugs. "I don't know — did you hear about how Nadia was hassling Kate about her thesis?" I know I shouldn't gossip with students about other faculty, but Nadia's such a bully. At every department meeting she brainstorms — in front of me — strategies for finding my replacement. "No, what happened," I say to the student feigning as little interest as possible. "Well, Nadia was going on and on about how Kate was going to have to do all these radical revisions to her poems, so Kate went home and changed the font — that's all, everything else she left the same — and gave it back to Nadia, and Nadia looked at it and said *much better* and approved it." We roll our eyes. Nadia's latest scheme is to lure in Barbara Kingsolver for a year. She met her for like five minutes at a cocktail party and refers to her as "Barbara" with this pushy familiarity. "Barbara is just what we need." (Sly glance to me who is just what they don't need.) "I'll give Barbara a call." Yeah, like Barbara Kingsolver would really come here for the money they offer. Some of us call Nadia the Iron Maiden.

And then the student does this weird thing — he lies down, throws his arms over his head and stretches out his body, all six big-boned feet of it. His boxy vintage shirt pulls up, revealing a flat hairy belly. He lets out a big yawn, rolls on his side and spreads his thighs wide open. Facing me. I don't say anything, but I feel awkward, swiveled around in my wooden office chair, his crotch the fulcrum of my vision, the blue gray cloth of his pants tugging across a cock I strain to avoid seeking the outlines of. His head and voice float somewhere above it. "Have you ever read *McSweeney's?*" He shifts around uncomfortably on the narrow bench, but his legs remain spread, his blue gray hips twisted toward me. "No, I've never seen it, what's it like?" No flirtation, no mention of his position, a couple of times he sneaks his hand down to cover something. "They're very much into irony—you, know, Dave Eggers." He acts so relaxed, as if his odalisque pose were a mere accident of positioning ass against bench. "I think irony has its limitations, don't you?" I wonder if his cock has hardened beneath that loose tent of fabric, would I know it, would it show?

I've never thought much about irony or the student's cock. Both exist in another dimension, far beyond the dense mists of The Personal, in a kind of Shangri-La that I am too old to enter. We talk often but mostly of writing. He knows more about me than I do about him. Can an eroticism so removed from acknowledgment be called eroticism at all? I have no desire to scoot closer, to touch him, but I can't stop peeking at the student's sprung tulip crotch. I imagine his balls hanging from his groin in net bags, a miniature Eva Hesse sculpture. He says, "I'm going to eat with you." Then he sits up, pulls an apple from his designer bicycle bag, lies back down, and spreads. He burnishes the apple on his blue gray inner thigh, holds it up for both of us to admire. It looks like a Pippin. Then he takes a big bite, his short thick fingers cramped around the shiny apple, the greenish sheen of its skin a fish eye reflecting the room. The student's skin is as pale as the apple flesh, pale as Vermeer's milkmaid, more ivory than pink. Moles spatter his creamy forearms. He stays up late, sleeps late, a creature who lives on books, coffee, and zinfandel. He likes to walk in snow at night, not that he's seen snow in years. Once he told me about the hairless white spiders of Thailand. His mouth half full of apple mush, he says, "My father is very aggressive." His Adam's apple bobs as he swallows. "He threatens people at airports." Brown chest curls peek through the V of his carelessly buttoned shirt. "To get good seats. You don't have to be working class to be violent." His father is five years older than I. I tell the student my father called me "it," as in "look at it sitting there," meaning me. "How old were you?" the student asks. "I don't know, late grade school."

The student's cock is the milk of my magnesia,
the magnetic milk of my amnesia.

I've always imagined that sociopaths make great teachers.
They're charismatic, stay focused. Nadia never says hello to me
in the hallway, she just struts past in her rumpled linen jackets
with her gaze averted. I've never done anything to her — except
get hired when she was on sabbatical. I've tried over and over
to show how subservient I am, how respectful, how *not a threat*.
This afternoon at the English Department tea I politely listened
for a full eight minutes about her latest performance piece,
"Salome and the Second Chakra," in which she apparently
recites poetry and does a belly dance in red veils. "Salome is
such a powerful feminist role model," she said, loud enough
for the whole room to hear. Then she turned her mane of black
curls from left to right, as if to note who dared not to listen.
"Salome wasn't afraid to express her sexuality, her appetites."
I kept trying to think of an engaged question to ask, something
about feminism or audience or how long she worked on it, but
nothing would come to mind. I was totally, fucking
thoughtless, like the engaged question generator in my brain
had been erased by powerful magnets. I stood there, holding
my paper cup of Earl Grey, grinning and nodding like a puppet
with a weak neck, the afternoon light glaring off the giant
amber beads of Nadia's necklace *poor little insects trapped in sap*.
I kept glancing at the chocolate thumbprint cookies heaped on
the table beside us. I wanted to stuff them in my mouth with
both fists. The student says, "Before you came here, all the hip
students hung around with Nadia, but now they're hanging
around you. She's jealous."

He shifts on the bench, thrusting his blue gray canopy of crotch
in the air. Spread thighs are such a feminine gesture, one that
reflects our power dynamics, I suppose. He splays himself
before me, vulnerable in my 3-D House of Wax. The camera
lingers on his dewy shoulders and face, his brown hair
cascading against the planks of the wooden casket I've
strapped him into. Thermostatic dials have been cranked up
and a vat of bubblegum pink wax bubbles wildly. Pink steam
singes his nostrils. The danger excites him. Spatial depth is

exaggerated in 3-D, ultralayered so that objects appear as fences in front of other objects. The student in his coffin is so clearly in front of the boiling wax, which is so clearly in front of the thermostatic dials. The wax maker's laboratory looks a mile deep. The camera sweeps from dials to vat to coffin, the student's cock pops up and the audience screams. It pokes out of the screen and into the Castro Theater, its gigantic ghostly head bobbing in the popcorn-scented air. Beneath it hundreds of gapes and giggles. His cock is creaming, its white beads of cum radiant, as if glowing from within. The guy behind me squeals, "This is *so* good."

I walk the student to the door. It's difficult to stand so close to him, his luminescent pearl flesh sucking up the room's light. He reaches out and gently touches my arm with a finger. "See you." The student's cock is a small bird struggling. If I should die as I held it in my hands, a fine white mist would poof up from my palm, a fine white flame dissolving in the air. My office feels so empty. Outside my window ornate iron lampposts brighten the mild suburban night. I pull down the shades and return to my desk. On the bulletin board beside it hangs a parchment with a quote by Barbara Kingsolver, written in calligraphy: "When a poem does arrive I gasp as if an apple had fallen into my hand." It's illustrated with a rather Japanese-looking brush-stroked apple. I click open the Vermeer file.

> Dusk sneaks softly like a bandit through my office
> window.
> *Too right and too beautiful* wrote Eva Hesse,
> *I'd like to do a little more wrong.*
> Semen drips from the dark hole, a river
> of cum. The milkmaid pours impassively,
> but inside she's a dark vat
> of passion and pain.
> The pitcher is her cunt, milky cunt
> juices spewing into the unknown.
> The radiant light from the Dutch window
> white as milk cum.

The jug is an open mouth,
a baby burping, an old crone's dribble.
She regurgitates white, she dies
old toothless and drooling, still an adjunct.
The milk shapeshifts and dazzles,
a hazy opium dream,
the molten lead Quasimodo poured
on the murderous peasants below,
pink steam streaming
from scorched screaming flesh.

Clarice, my officemate, bursts into the room. "Carla, you scared me! What are you doing here so late?" "Catching up." With her three-year contract Clarice is the queen bee of the visiting writer pool. She drops her DKNY briefcase on the bench and hands me a sheet of lined notepaper, ripped raggedly across the top. "Look what I found pinned to Nadia's door." In green marker is scrawled I SAW WHAT YOU DID LAST SOLSTICE. DIE IRON MAIDEN. "I took it down—not even Nadia deserves to come in and see this. I don't know what to do, destroy it, give it to the dean. Oh my god!" I look up from the note. She's pointing at my computer screen. "*The Milkmaid*! I love her, she's so sacred, yet so commonplace." "I'm writing a Vermeer poem," I say. "For Bob's section?" I nod. "So am I. Have you seen my other Vermeer poem—on *Lady Writing a Letter*?" She darts over to her briefcase and pulls out the latest issue of *Magnificat*. "Here—page 53. Vermeer is so awesome," she continues, adjusting the silk scarf, deep crimson, that's draped about her gaunt neck. "I assigned him to my seminar 'Poetry and the Visual.' 'Write a Vermeer poem,' I told them. The students are very excited."

Notes From the Field:
The 2000 Republican Convention

Day 1

I'm writing this on an iBook, and a tangerine one at that, on my mother's kitchen table. I'm just finishing the end of my first of three weeks in Indiana. My background reading on the convention has been from the *Lake County Times.* One columnist would have preferred Rush Limbaugh to Bush, but he admits that most of the country doesn't feel that way. He goes on to praise Bush's choice of Cheney as running mate: people think Bush is stupid, so it's brilliant of him to choose a running mate perceived as smarter than he is. When I mention Cheney to Kevin on the phone, he gasps, "Cheney invented the Gulf War." Kevin suggests I read something more liberal—like *Time* magazine.

But I don't, and the next day I read how Gore will eat away at our civil liberties—like our right to bear arms and to free speech—and that at Clinton's directive the FBI is monitoring all the emails of an unnamed internet service provider—and the provider isn't allowed to tell its clients. Hello! Where's this information coming from? Conspiracy dot com? Outer space?

My mother works on a crossword puzzle during most of the convention. When Colin Powell brags about Texas students' improved test scores during Bush's gubernatorial reign, my mother looks up from her puzzle and says, "Those are big numbers he's throwing around. Them numbers don't mean shit. Twelve students could have improved." My mother adds that if Colin Powell were president, she'd feel that everything would be all right, that he makes you feel safe, that you can trust him. Colin Powell gets paid big bucks for giving speeches, and it's easy to see why. The only line of his I laughed out loud at was the one about two million "convicts—not consumers." The alliteration, and the suggestion that freedom equals consumption equals human value.

People are protesting outside the convention, but the news gives no details, and from here in Indiana, it's hard to understand what they're protesting about. We've got these really nice people up there promoting diversity and education with choreographed sincerity. (It reminds me of my grant-writing days.) The last Republican convention was choreographed too, but cartoony, fun to watch and laugh at — as long as you didn't think of these right-wing warmongers ruling the world. They were scary, and that's why Dole didn't win, the Republicans scared the shit out of people. These new Republicans aren't scary and that's what really scares me. Laura Bush seems like a nice middle class lady. I miss Libby Dole, her vulgarity, her pizzazz, her bright yellow suit. I predict that this evening when she appears, we'll be greeted with a toned-down Libby, a Libby so bland she might as well be a Democrat.

Day 2

Almost all the coverage in Tuesday's paper is from the Associated Press. As I sip my coffee I read over and over how the Republican convention is trying to co-opt the look and issues of the Democrats. I also learn that the platform is still firmly anti-abortion, and the position against gay rights has been strengthened. Beneath all the niceness, the predator still stalks. I think of a dozen alien invasion movies, and the giant insects in *Mimic*. I know it and entomologist Mira Sorvino knows it too: the figure may look human, act human, but there always comes the glory shot when the smiling surface dissolves and the gooey bug brain flashes.

Indiana makes me horny. I keep having fantasies of fucking a construction worker. In the afternoon I cruise around in my mother's Chevy Cavalier, blasting the classic rock station, the Rolling Stones, "Wild Horses." I peek in the rearview mirror at the guy behind me in the blue pickup pouring coffee from a thermos, and my heart is filled with pure lust.

My mother and I have agreed to watch the convention between

nine and ten (Central Time), when the headliners speak. My brother and his wife drop by unexpectedly at about quarter to nine, and I think, this should be fun. My brother yells to me in the kitchen, where I'm washing dishes. My apron is white, decorated with chefs' heads done in liquid embroidery, which is like a permanent magic marker. Without my glasses it looks like real embroidery. "So what kind of car do you drive in San Francisco? Is it a foreign car?" he snorts. "No," I snap back. "I own a 1987 Dodge Aries wagon, an American car that was so shitty there aren't many of them left around." My brother's job as a crane operator in one of the few remaining steel mills is under constant threat. Expanded global trade is never going to fly around here.

Finally, what I've been waiting for, glorious theme music swells as Libby Dole takes the stage. "I hate that music," says my sister-in-law. Everybody agrees. "What movie was that music from—the one where they carried the torches—I hated that movie too—running along the beach with the torches—it won an Academy Award—and so did the song—I hate that song—now what movie was it—this is going to drive me nuts." Libby's not very interesting in her pale blue suit, empty platitudes, she's trying to be the new whatever the Republicans are being this year, but nothing will ever be new about Libby. *Chariots of Fire*, my brother announces proudly. "Thank you." It's agreed that lots of movies win Academy Awards that don't deserve it—like *Fargo* and *American Beauty*. But, *Sling Blade*, that was a good one.

As John McCain speaks I'm told they tortured him for five years in Vietnam, but there's disagreement whether or not he "signed the paper." My mother says he signed it, but regrets it. All agree that after five years of torture, you can't hold it against a guy for signing. My mother says all they'd have to do is twist her little finger and she'd sign. Nobody respects McCain for backing Bush. "A few days ago Bush was the worst shit, and now they're good friends. I don't trust none of them."

My mother points toward the TV, "He's got a weird neck." I'd been noticing how saggy McCain's neck is too, compared to his taut face. "His face looks like one of them masks they rip off in movies, like the face is a mask." She grabs the right side of her face with her left hand, as if she were going to rip it off. "See?" My brother laughs, "He probably hung himself from losing so many times." I try to listen to what McCain is saying while my brother tells my mother about the live turkey farm that's only thirty-five minutes away. "They'll let you break its neck yourself, if you want to." The turkeys are in bins by weight, and some of them weigh forty pounds. "It would take three days to cook that son of a bitch."

Day 3

My mother is having a good day today, so we visit her friend Stella. Stella used to live across the street, but around the same time I was entering puberty, she built a much bigger house in a better neighborhood. I still have dreams of knocking on the front door of her tiny gray shingled one-story. "Can Mike and Pat come out to play?" Her husband worked at an oil refinery and painted houses on the side, he worked all the time and invested money, and now Stella is a millionaire. Her new house is decorated with lace doilies and antique china. As we sit in her living room drinking caffeine-free Pepsi, Stella tells us about the guy next door who's fucking crazy, how he tried to run down the high school kid across the street, how one time the crazy fuck mooned her and she got to see his fucking weenie. She turns to me and laughs, "Oh, I guess I shouldn't be talking this way in front of you, I shouldn't be using those words." I say, "You forget who raised me," meaning my carpenter father. My mom says, "You'd think when Barney started working in the schools, he'd talk better, but he talked dirtier than ever. Them educated people cuss more than anybody else." "Educated people!" I guffaw. "He hung out with football coaches and shop teachers." "He'd be in the teachers' lounge," my mother continues, "and you should have heard some of the jokes them women teachers told him. I'd be embarrassed to talk that way in front of a man. You wouldn't believe how them educated people talk." My mother doesn't know much about my life, but she knows I teach college.

Where the hell do I fit in here? McCain is not the only one, I fear, whom she sees with a masked face. Them educated people.

When I was in high school we were in a constant state of battle over housework. She was always after me to scrub the bathroom, and I wanted to spend all my time being a teen intellectual. A clean house was a moral imperative. If Shirley Jackson had written my mother's life, women with piles of dirty laundry on the floor would be stoned. So, now that I'm helping out as she recovers from her operation, she's appalled at my incompetence. "You whish that broom around like you ain't never touched a floor before." When I vacuumed her living room the other day, I complained about her vacuum, a thirty-year-old Filter Queen that wore me out. "You should get an upright, where you just walk behind it and it sort of moves itself across the floor." "The kids, and then Stella said the same thing, complaining about it. That's a good vacuum. You all just don't know how to vacuum." My brother and his wife are "the kids," but I'm just Dodie. I feel a pang of jealousy. The vacuum comes up at Stella's, and Stella says how terrible it is, how my mother should get an upright. "One of them uprights won't pick up cat fur and dust on a kitchen floor." "Yes it will, I can get mine out and show you." "No it won't. You all just don't know how to vacuum." My mother used to work part-time as a janitress. There's no dishonor in a bit of elbow grease. "Winnie, you ain't never going to change your mind about that stupid vacuum—you're just like Betty, her being a Democrat! She'd vote for anybody they threw up there." Stella sweeps her arm up and our eyes follow. "You ain't supposed to vote for the party, you're supposed to vote for the man."

Day 4

Thursday night is our chance to see the man, the acceptance speech of George W. Bush. I nibble on cold pizza and my mother eats animal crackers. Just the two of us. Cozy. When Bush co-opts the civil rights cry "We Shall Overcome," I think, this man has no limits. My mother heckles the TV. "You can't believe that bull. Every election, it's the same shit. You can't believe them. I don't believe them." When Bush brags about all the accomplishments of Texas, "and we blah blahed and we blah blahed," my mother yells out, "And we killed plenty of people." I guess she's against the death penalty. She tells me that Florida and Texas kill more people than any other states.

Bush is doing a great job. The audience doesn't seem hung up on his weird alliterative lines, such as the presidency "turns pride into prayer." Neither my mother nor I can figure out what the fuck that means. The camera closes in on teary eye after teary eye. Mostly women. (He is kind of cute, with his compact features and sly eyes—the way he and Laura look at each other announces Good Sex.) Political speech turns into revival meeting. Bush is speaking to a spiritual crisis that is breaking America apart. People want healing, and he's anointing them. "It won't be long...it won't be long."

The camera cuts to a mask of Bush on a wooden stick, just a cutout photo of his face floating and bobbing, with holes for eyes. The red dress and thick pearls of the woman behind show through the hollow eyes. "Look at that," I exclaim. "Yeck," says my mother. "That's creepy!" Bush says, "God Bless America," and thousands of balloons fall. They look like animated scrubbing molecules in a soap commercial. Bush walks among his following, hugging, and kissing. My mother shouts, "Watch out for kissing those girls, Georgie. One of them might show you her thong!"

LA-Kevin

If you log on to LA-Kevin's live webcam, chances are he's naked, whether he's watching TV, cooking pasta, taking a dump, installing his new VCR, or fucking. The only time I see him in clothes is when he's getting ready to go out or cleaning his glassed-in patio. His boyfriend, Rufus, is usually snuggled beneath the covers, his shaved head and perhaps a tattooed bicep showing, while Kevin sleeps fully exposed beside him. The purple bedspread is a riot of stylized leafy fragments, like an Art Deco jungle. Kevin looks so feral stretched out on top of it, a long albino panther, his cock in a gentle arc falling to the left. In the three years that it's been up, LA-Kevin's site has received a million and a half hits. Through email and chat rooms, fans approach him nervously as if he were a star. "I don't get that," says LA-Kevin. "I'm just a normal guy in an apartment in West Hollywood."

"Normal" in West Hollywood is a different bag of marbles than in most places. Originally a Prohibition boomtown, West Hollywood was incorporated as a city in 1984 and remains proudly outside the grip of the LAPD. Its go-go nightlife still rollicks full force in the clubs clustered along Sunset Strip — the Whiskey Bar, Trocadero, Ciro's, Mocambo. LA-Kevin lives in an 18-unit building on the east side of this mecca for gays, Russians, hedonistic celebrities, and all kinds of outcasts. His apartment is always online, 24-7, always available to me for free, like nature or the ideal lover. I come home after a stressful day, open a beer and log on. In this era of confessional talk shows and reality TV I'm used to strangers glad to be intimate with me. On the web you don't have to wait for Geraldo to invite you. Cameras are cheap. Anybody with the tiniest amount of expendable income can erupt from the passivity of audience and leap inside the picture tube. I sip my beer and Kevin jacks off. I watch him complacently as I would tropical fish.

Kevin, who works as a computer technologist, is disdainful of the "consumer-grade" cameras used on most sites. At their worst the resolution is so poor that people lurch through a blur of lurid magentas and purples, like a bad acid flashback. Over the past three years, Kevin has rigged up a network of seven professional security cameras with remote controls to switch between them. In the bedroom there's one in the ceiling for a "bird's-eye view." Another is set up next to the bed. The third one's portable. He usually places it in front of himself when he sits at his computer, but he also moves it around the bedroom or takes it to other parts of the apartment. There's two more in the bathroom and another in the kitchen. His boyfriend can't sleep with the lights on, so Kevin bought an infrared camera, which can broadcast in the dark when Rufus sleeps over. The infrared images appear in black and white, but it's worth it to keep Rufus happy. Kevin's thoughtful like that. If a guest objects to being filmed, he'll either move with them to another room or switch the feed to another camera. "Hey, the rule is this is life, and life is about people, that's what's important. So if the people in my life are made uncomfortable by the presence of the camera then I need to cater to the comfort of my friends."

Though every room has been online at one time or another, I've never seen the living room or dining area. "Do you plan to go into the living room sometime soon?" I hint. "Yes," says LA-Kevin. "I'd really be interested in seeing those rooms." Kevin says, "I get what you're getting at," but unlike some camera operators, he doesn't take requests. "In chat rooms we get hammered with requests from people who demand that we perform, almost like circus animals." For Kevin living his life "on cam" means dropping self-consciousness, forgetting about the camera's presence. He can always switch cameras if he needs to retreat, but he doesn't need to very often. "Most people are amazed I don't feel invaded. But most people have only experienced cameras under a situation of being monitored." He read an article that said your face is photographed an average of six times an hour when you're out and about doing your daily duties. "I'm not being monitored. I'm totally in control of what's being shown and what's being seen." Kevin's adamant that he's not an exhibitionist. "The camera is simply present when I'm living life here at home, so sex is not outside of that." He's been a nudist all his life. As a teen when his parents went out for the evening, he'd take his clothes off and do his chores, watch TV, play the piano. Anything done without clothes excited him. He didn't know there was a community out there until seven years ago when he joined a Los Angeles nudist club. The gay male club mostly holds movie nights and cocktails in members' homes. Occasionally they'll rent out a restaurant, or a play with onstage nudity, or a Palm Springs resort.

As Kevin hunches over his boyfriend's chest and kisses him, suddenly the video slows down to a halt. Briefly the picture disappears altogether. Other viewers have caught on to their having sex and the network is overloaded. Our hunger for images jams the system. In this space sex is inevitable. That's what keeps us watching. Like crime scene photos, even when unpopulated the rooms feel charged. Webcam never gives the illusion of fluid "natural" movement. It's more like a series of stills that jerk into the next still. Kevin's empty bedroom twitches as the camera refreshes, so it appears to be alive, to be breathing. The kite-shaped leaves on the bedspread rustle. We sense the sacred and profane jostling in this stillness which is never really still. When Kevin enters the space, his body feels like a prop within the bedroom's languorous aloneness. Events break down into a series of mini-events, and the jumps between them evade the narrative pressure of our central nervous system. We sit in our office chairs exalting in their mystery. A hand strobes along a cock. Blink. White stuff spews out of it, caught in midair like a Muybridge horse. We're never sure what we're missing. Light through the venetian blinds stripes both the bed and Kevin. He looks half mummy, half tiger.

Watching this stuff is banal and tedious as hanging out at the mall. It's quickly addictive. Warhol would have loved the webcam. Kevin's apartment sprawls out before us, labyrinthine genitalia that keep unfolding. We zoom in on the details with the tenderness of a stalker—the remote and cellphone beside him on the bed, his white crew socks, the giant RCA dog "Nipper" he dusts on the patio. What I would give to read the clippings on Kevin's refrigerator door. If you watch regularly, it's exciting to see new rooms, new angles appear. Fans are always asking Kevin about the objects in his bedroom, and he's generous with his answers. While he loves porn, what he's usually watching on TV are shows taped with TiVo, "an amazing tool in the way it allows you to control your TV viewing experience." Control is important to Kevin. Those two photos hanging on the wall beside the dresser, right above the wastepaper basket, are pages from an early '80s Soloflex home gym brochure. Kevin ripped them out and framed them. "It was the guy that I thought had the most perfect body. When I'm in bed I can look over and see them there at the right height. It's something that was done exclusively for myself." The picture above the TV has a "sparkly black background with golden sparkly things behind it, there are holes cut out in the blackness to make out one of the bridges in San Francisco." The lava lamp beneath it used to be green, but sitting in the sun it turned gold, so Kevin moved it to pick up the gold in the bridge. That weird futuristic painting above the bed is a print embossed on wood. He purchased it in a furniture store because he liked the colors. It's the kind of picture, he confides, where they tell you it's the last one, but then you come back the following week and there's another one hanging in the exact same place.

Kevin's decor is functional, masculinist, its colors bold yet subdued. It could be the home of any gay man with a credit card. He's unapologetic about his Ikea furniture. "I'm very much a mainstream shopper." "Is that a Noguchi lamp by the bed?" "I can assure you it is not." The mass-market look of the bedroom furniture, the cheap boxy modernity of the particleboard cabinets in the kitchen further fuel our fantasies. Kevin's nakedness is hot, not just because he's got a big cock, but because it removes specificity. As the weekend progresses, clothes are strewn across the floor and bed, an open dresser drawer spills its contents, the nightstand is cluttered with bottles and tubes. We don't know what's in the bottles, we can't make out the drawer's contents, and the clothes are unassuming pants and shirts. The more disheveled the interiors, the sexier they become. Clearer details would be an intrusion. This is the messiness of ordinary life, the terrain of the Polaroid snapshot. There's an illusion of the unmediated in the way we experience this naked body moving from room to room. In a space this minimal, anything goes. Whenever he's home the bedroom TV is on, its fuzzy picture jerking in time to the room's breathing. Kevin, seduced by images, seduces us with images. We're engaged in an endless cycle of ingestion and expulsion. In the bathroom the naked body shaves its balls, in the kitchen it lingers beside an electric stove, the glowing coils and boiling water disturbingly close to vulnerable flesh.

The environment gives so little it lures us back, again and again. We cling to it through the narratives we create. Kevin is in bed with another man. The man is lying on his stomach on the side of the bed farthest away from the camera. Kevin rolls and twitches, the full length of his naked body exposed. The other guy is so still he may be dead. Does he know about the camera? They wake late and have sex for hours. Elliot and I watch them in San Francisco. Elliot says they must be party boys. What drugs could create such potency? Kevin sets his sneakers on the bed after sex, and Elliot exclaims, "The guys are going to the gym!" Rufus, with his shaved head, packs a suitcase and Jack in Canada writes in Kevin's guest book that Rufus must be in the military. Kevin thinks it's natural for people to create stories for him. "It's like watching a silent movie that you know has an audio track and wasn't meant to be a silent movie. It's like half of it's missing, your mind is going to want to fill in the holes." Mostly his viewers imagine true love. In Kevin's guest book Jackson from Kentucky writes, "I only wish I could find someone like these two guys, always touching when together in bed. I'd move about anywhere for that kind of love." Barry from Canada adds, "There is a god and Kevin gets the love he needs and deserves." Not surprisingly, Kevin feels warmth for the people who watch him. "I feel comforted having the camera around. I'm never alone. When I come home there's always somebody here. Whenever I want to interface with the people who watch, it's a pleasant experience. They're the perfect roommate. They're not messing up the place, and I have companionship that I'm not troubled by."

Not Clinical, But Probable

for John Wieners

His teeth were rotting; his matted hair stuck out like an irregular porcupine; I was twenty-four and unblemished and I fucked his brains out because he recited Yeats as we watched the sun rise over San Francisco's skyline from his big smelly bed. Besides, he was a professional poet—even his caked fingernails were numinous.

The night we met he drove me home with a kiss and a copy of his book. Neither of us would admit the route to my building so the five minute drive took half an hour. A few days later I called him from my drafting table at Wells Fargo Bank (I didn't last there long because of the rip in the ass of my jeans), "Hi, I had a dream about you." He knew I wanted to fuck so he said, "How about Saturday around dinner?"

When I got to his place I just couldn't. He was forty years old and started to cry, so I hugged him. *Putty warm and forbidden because the boundaries were olfactory and therefore fleeting—a chemical change in my perceptions as if sinking right through his plaid shirt to something dark and confusing like molasses without its stick...*Afterwards I was starving but he offered me no food.

The remembrance of a body odor—after ten years there is only recognition cultivated or avoided. Schizophrenic: I sniff one in an elevator, toenails so long they curl back into his feet. The smell of a brain on fire or some deep molecular awakening like the children at the end of *The Four-Gated City;* I bet their armpits had a distinctly pungent aroma.

Naked before his elevator door he did a jig and serenaded me on his guitar. See how his hairy jewels jingle like loose change.

He didn't have a kitchen table so I sprawled on his bed in my purple drawstring pants, black leotard and white overblouse with Bambi embroidered on the left pocket. I had a Mary

Travers hairdo—blonde to the middle of my back and bangs. Surrounded by empty bookcases I stared at the one with the plastic nativity scene on top, hoping that this time "dinner" meant food. The Virgin Mary's face was peeling when he emerged from the kitchen with two plates covered by raw steak. The red secretion against the white china reminded me of my period but at least the blood between my thighs was warm. He took a huge bite, tiny crimson bubbles beading his lower lip. Maybe if I was starving in the Arctic...I set it on the floor and looked out the window not really seeing anything. He said, "How about some peanut butter?" and brought out a jar of Skippy and a spoon.

Holding his breath he puckered his lips then released them with a quick forceful exhalation and said there wasn't any difference between fearing execution and being executed.

> blood is the water-
>   color
> they use to turn on.

The traffic outside sounded like an ocean with an occasional honk. Hotel room on Kearny and Broadway—he would stay there for a week or two, his version of a cottage in Vermont. The bars and neon lights flashed new synapses in a tired mind. That night he wore one of those thick cream-colored sweaters from Ireland—Fisherman's knit—because his favorite Bible story was the King Fisher. When he took it off we made love on the sagging twin bed. No sheet on the thin blue-striped mattress...two images kept intruding upon my carnal pleasure: "prison cell" and "lice." A sink dripped in the corner and an old Italian coughed in the next room. We were doing it missionary but don't think this moment was conservative. His fucking was as messy as his clothes; sometimes he would murmur, "You have a delicious body" and I felt like I was being slurped. His rhythm was more of a spiral than they typical push-pull. But it worked—I would come lying on my back, legs spread wide; I've never done that with anyone else. It's frightening that way—nothing to grab onto *a line was inching down my navel and when it hit my clit it would split open spilling forth a mass of gleaming red à la Cronenberg* I was holding my breath thinking, "I can't stand it" when he said, "Come on my dear, come for me." And I did but I was so pissed I was a grenade wanting to blow his cock off—how dare he interfere with my moment.

I wrote him on ice colored paper in an ice colored envelope, "I'm the girl of the ballads—alive or ghostly my long plait of hair getting wet on the moors, it only happens once and then you die, but that can be multiple too like an orgasm but you wouldn't know because being male you're not supposed to have them or do you?"

He sat in his wooden arm chair and smoked two cigarettes at a time, one in each hand his head rocking back and forth. I was silent as I watched cross-legged from his bed. The sheets had never been washed, all gray and smelling not so much funky as strange—as if the essence of schizophrenia had been extracted into a perfume like your own armpits or gas, something repulsive that you want to inhale.

I am infused with the day even tho the day may destroy me.

Fingering the scars on his naked body, the frail ones on wrist throat cheek knee; pink fissures too smooth for skin, polished and therefore a conversation piece. *There are bandages on the wounds/ but blood flows unabated.* Everything is self-inflicted: autopsy ridges across his pale and softly heaving chest.

He was starving so he wrote lean poems. Sipping Jack Daniel's from a champagne glass, he said the only reason he was alive was because he didn't know enough anatomy to find his jugular vein.

I sat on the toilet blue jeans wrinkled around my ankles, staring at my pink bikini panties the cotton crotch stained from some period of unknown date or origin—its simple vulnerability reminded me of him. *I had love once in the palm of my hand. See the lines there.* My body was operating according to principles it wasn't communicating to me: I craved the taste of sulphur, my chest broke out in hives whenever I heard The Beach Boys, especially "Surfin' Safari." And it dawned on me a realization so obvious it could have been my mother: NATURAL LAWS ARE JUST A STATE OF MIND. If this were a movie there would be swirling colors and I would take on the facial characteristics of an ape. *Again to smell what this calm ocean cannot tell us.* Raising his head from between my thighs his cheeks glistening, he sniffed and said, "My dear you're going to make a *great* poet!"

He always played the fool, the innocent...his mouth an *O* like an anus and smelling as bad, a big belly laugh, "And Ferlinghetti had to sit there and take it because everybody in the room knew I was *crazy!*"

We sat at his "desk," a blonde picnic bench lit by this grotesquely smiling ovum a foot wide: blue jacket red bow tie, perched on the proverbial wall. Humpty Dumpty. I kept thinking *humanoid but not quite born.* A former wife had found it in a thrift store. That, a Guatemalan blanket, and the poems he incessantly dedicated to her were the sum total of her remains. He handed me his latest, blue ballpoint on lined paper ripped from a spiral binder, the script shaky as if written with the wrong hand, each three-lined stanza creeping a little farther to the right. I could make out 75% of it and one complete thought: "We lived near the East river over/ a laundromat, taking the West bound bus/ to work. Glory and the grand illusory spectacles." Lit by that glowing bald dome his own hair poked out like a crown (he always looked like he was still in bed), brown wisps stuck to his beaded forehead, sweat so profuse a person could drink from his frontal lobe. He had removed his glasses preferring the world blurred—it helped him be crazy. After all, that was his profession; any visible signs of improvement could cost him thousands a year. But that wasn't likely, not as often as he was committed—for running naked down Haight Street or driving on the grass of Golden Gate Park with a 4-year-old friend steering the wheel. He wouldn't sleep for six weeks and then he'd be rolling around the hospital floor; he begged them not to but the doctors gave him drugs that made him howl like a bear with its foot crushed in a rusty metal mouth.

> *After all, I am possessed*
> *by wild animals and*
> *long haired men and*
> *women who gallop*
> *breaking over my beloved*
> *places.*

He summed up his theory of poetics in a single word: confusion.

He was 365 years old, having met a magician in the Black Forest who gave him eternal life. But that didn't mean he couldn't be murdered. There were voices on the radio plotting his destruction. We were in bed together, a sudden clamp around my arm, his fingers squeezing to bruise, he sat up, "You believe me, don't you?" Nodding furiously, "Of course I believe I understand I mean why not?"

I wrote on pink paper in a pale blue envelope: "It's all about an edge to be up against."

> *And yet, we must remember.*
> *The old forest, the wild*
> *screams in the backyard*
> *or cries in the bedroom.*

Rocking back and forth, the way blind people are taught not to do he gave a shrill laugh then froze suddenly, a statue with darting brown eyes. His jeans were baggy and his green turtleneck stained. I thought the hair matted out in all directions from lack of washing, but once I was there when he shampooed — it automatically dried in the same neo-expressionistic configuration.

After his reading at Intersection he met a woman, and barely so she being nineteen and the kind that throws her long brown hair in her face to hide something ordinary like a nose or an idea. When she paid for his book with a Susan B. Anthony silver dollar he called me up, "That means she's a feminist and wants to kill me!"

Their long hair binds them,

They have lain long
hours in bed, blood
on their mouths, arms
reaching down for
ground not given them.

His friends were over and I was embarrassed to be the only person in the room who had never attempted suicide. If you really want to succeed you slice the vein up the arm and not across. Otherwise you wake up in the psych ward your hands numb and unable to withstand the pressure of a pencil, though typing is all right for a short while. He was always rushing his friends off to the hospital. Once when he drove up to Mendocino to rescue a fighting couple he couldn't decide if it was proper to take them to different hospitals or the same one.

I wrote him on beige paper in a yellow envelope, "You drink your friends' sadness like wine but it's not clear if you like the taste." But I didn't mean his friends, I meant me.

He autographed his book in black ink framing the words with little hearts and musical notes:

"For Dodie —
      'a young frost
      makes her first sketches
      on the panes of my cabin'
   A great writer and a true love
   from now until heaven — "

Linda Betty had been in therapy since she was born. When her divorce was finalized she was so depressed she wanted to sleep with me. Fingering my hair in the supermarket line she blurted out, "Dodie, let's start a lesbian nation." So I said, "Go over and fuck him and he'll tell you you're a good writer." She did and he did and it was obvious he liked her better than me. She would take her clothes off and run around his apartment yelling, "Don't try to touch me. Right now I just can't deal with sex!" He would follow her, begging. Neither one of them knew the difference between static and a wavelength.

The poem/ does not lie to us. We lie under/ its laws, alive in the glamour of this hour…

I write as if this didn't bother me. Not true—I found it disgusting. But it had its moments. I was "in love" with him—at twenty-four I could still tell a person that. Any more I'd rather have my lips fall off. I was also in various stages of affairs with Bruce Nance Gary and Lynn. My love was totally devoid of understanding and therefore limitless. He said I had the typical attitude of a young poet—life wasn't something to live but to devour. My conversation was a barrage of details each one more sparkling than the last. He would occasionally interrupt to say, "That's a good line." He made me feel so special my jaws cramped from smiling.

> *That love is my strength, that*
> *I am overpowered by it:*
> > *desire*
> > > *that too*
> *is on the face: gone stale.*

One evening our conversation was boring in a subtle sort of way—he was plotting his next letter to Ken Kesey or calculating which relatives if any had money to leave him—and I realized a crazy person can be mundane. Suddenly the enchantment was broken and I had the fishy taste in my mouth you get from kissing a frog. There was no need for him to leave me, but he said I was the kind of girl a man would have to marry and he could never do that. At that time marriage was like pregnancy, a physical impossibility, so I never bothered with birth control or hiding my feelings. Boy was I in for a big surprise…

Dodie Bellamy has written a novel, *The Letters of Mina Harker* (University of Wisconsin Press, 2004) and an epistolary collaboration on AIDS with the late Sam D'Allesandro, *Real* (Talisman House, 1994). Her book, *Cunt-Ups* (Tender Buttons, 2002), a radical feminist revision of the "cut-up" pioneered by William Burroughs and Brion Gysin, won the 2002 Firecracker Alternative Book Award for Poetry. Her work has appeared in, among others, the anthologies *Pills, Thrills, Chills and Heartache*, *The Best American Erotica 2001*, *High Risk*, *The Art of Practice: 45 Contemporary Poets*, *A Poetics of Criticism*, *The New Fuck You*, *Primary Trouble*, and *Moving Borders: Three Decades of Innovative Writing by Women*. In 1998 she won the San Francisco Bay Guardian "Goldie" Award for Literature. Her essays and book reviews have appeared in *The Village Voice*, *The San Francisco Chronicle*, *Bookforum*, *Out/Look*, *The San Diego Reader*, *Nest*, as well as numerous small press literary journals and websites. She has taught creative writing at the San Francisco Art Institute, Mills College, UC Santa Cruz, University of San Francisco, Naropa University, Antioch Los Angeles, San Francisco State, and CalArts. With Kevin Killian, she has edited over 100 issues of the literary/art zine *Mirage #4/Period(ical)*.